Garyck's Gift

RAYNA TYLER

Copyright © 2022 Rayna Tyler

All rights reserved. No part of this publication may be reproduced, stored in a retrieval system, or transmitted, in any form or by any means, without the prior written permission of the author.

This is a work of fiction. Names, characters, places, and incidents are either the product of the author's imagination or are used fictitiously, and any resemblance to actual persons living or dead, business establishments, events, or locales, is entirely coincidental.

ISBN: 978-1-953213-30-3

ALSO BY RAYNA TYLER

Seneca Falls Shifters

Tempting the Wild Wolf
Captivated by the Cougar
Enchanting the Bear
Enticing the Wolf
Teasing the Tiger

Ketaurran Warriors

Jardun's Embrace
Khyron's Claim
Zaedon's Kiss
Rygael's Reward
Logan's Allure
Garyck's Gift

Crescent Canyon Shifters

Engaging His Mate
Impressing His Mate

Bradshaw Bears

Bear Appeal

CHAPTER ONE

SLOANE

I settled on the bench beside the long rectangular table in the gathering room of the rebel headquarters, relaxing as I took in my surroundings. The building wasn't fancy. Like everything else in the community, it had been designed for shelter and efficiency. The wooden walls might be bare and the furniture handcrafted, but the place was home. And after spending several weeks away, I was glad to be back.

I enjoyed staying at the drezdarr's dwelling in Aztrashar, one of the largest cities on Ketaurrios, but no matter how many times Laria, Celeste, and I made the trip, I couldn't wait to leave the place and return to the settlement.

The two females and I had been friends even before the *Starward Bounty*, our Earth exploration spaceship, had crash-landed and stranded its human survivors on this planet. Celeste sat across from Laria at the other end of the table, explaining what she'd planned for her upcoming wedding.

Celeste's mate Khyron, the drezdarr and ruler of the

planet, was sitting next to her. His blue eyes, a paler shade than the scales covering his arms, chest, and tail, flickered with interest as he listened to their conversation.

Thrayn, Zaedon, and his mate Cara, another close female friend, were the only others in the room. Cara and Zaedon were leaning against the wall near the main door. And, as usual, Thrayn had positioned himself not far from Khyron. He was the newest person to join the vryndarr, the elite warriors who served as bodyguards for the planet's ruler. Thrayn could be a bit overzealous in his duties, which sometimes annoyed Khyron and amused the rest of us.

Ketaurrans didn't have elaborate mating ceremonies, but now that Celeste was the drezdarrina, the celebration was a gift, Khyron's way of honoring human traditions.

I thought weddings were overrated and preferred the ketaurran way of doing things, so I was only half-listening to what Celeste was saying while I sipped my cup of freegea. The bitter plant-based drink was the only thing that came close to tasting like the coffee back on Earth.

My thoughts had drifted to the latest challenge facing our team; finding the laser blasters that had been recently discovered in our spaceship's wreckage and preventing the possibility of another war.

The last and only conflict I'd ever been pulled into had been brutal. It started shortly after Khyron's father welcomed us to their planet, offered us places to live in the cities, and helped us build homes in several settlements.

Sarus, Khyron's uncle, wanted to rule. His hatred of the humans fueled his desire and attempt to overthrow his brother. If it hadn't been for Burke, the rebel's leader, my friends and I might not have survived. He trained us to fight with our bodies and to wield any number of blades. Survival was difficult enough without having to deal with a planet-encompassing battle.

Many of the planet's inhabitants possessed excellent crafting skills but lacked the ability to construct advanced weaponry. Designing blades in various styles was the extent of their knowledge, which made confiscating the blasters so critical.

The ketaurran's weren't the only ones that produced despicable individuals who lacked respect for another being's life. A human mercenary named Doyle was responsible for finding the weapons after turning the ship into his personal compound. We'd recently learned that he'd sold the weapons to a ketaurran whose identity we were still trying to uncover.

We'd also discovered that he'd kept some for himself, an underhanded feat that had gotten his throat cut. Not only were we searching for the weapons he'd sold, but we also had to find the ones he'd kept. The males who'd worked for him had gone into hiding and taken the blasters with them, making our job even more difficult.

Worrying about our newest mission wasn't the only thing distracting me. The other was Garyck, an elite ketaurran warrior, one of the drezdarr's bodyguards, and another member of our team. The male had stolen my heart, something I hadn't openly shared with anyone, including my friends. Knowing me the way they did, I was certain they already knew how I felt about him.

Having no idea if Garyck felt the same way or what was currently going on with him was the source of my stress. Unless I'd imagined it, there was definitely chemistry between us. At one point, if asked, I'd been sure I meant something to him. But lately, and for some unknown reason, things had changed, and he'd been doing his best to avoid me.

Unlike humans who got together based on attraction, ketaurrans could actually recognize their mates by smell. Garyck had sniffed me enough times to know whether or not I was his ketiorra. We'd been working together for months. Since he hadn't said anything to me yet, I was certain we weren't meant to be together, no matter how badly I wished it were otherwise.

"Are you sure moving forward with the wedding is such a good idea?" Laria asked, tucking a honey blonde strand that had pulled loose from her braid behind her ear.

"Yes," Khyron said, smiling at Celeste. "Not only will a celebration help alleviate the tensions between the races, but it will show everyone we are serious about uniting everyone."

It was a good plan, one that would be destroyed if we didn't find the weapons. Something I was about to mention if Melissa hadn't opened the door leading outside and marched into the room. The ten-year-old was one of the orphans who lived with Harper and Rygael. Harper might not be a warrior, but she was fiercely protective of her friends and the children in her care.

Since Burke was in charge of the settlement, it wasn't uncommon for anyone living in the community to stop by the headquarters building without an invitation. The children were regular visitors.

Being in a room full of imposing adults armed with blades and ready to fight never seemed to bother any of them, Melissa included. She scanned the room, her brown eyes sparkling when they reached me. With determined steps, she closed the distance, then climbed on the bench next to me.

"Good morning, Melissa," I said, sipping from my cup while patiently waiting for her to state what was on her mind.

"Morning," she said, furrowing her brow, then taking a few seconds to choose her words. "Sloane." She patted my arm. "Can I ask you something?"

"Sure, what do you want to know?" I asked.

Melissa pinned me with a stern look. "Did you and Garyck break up?"

Surprised by her unexpected question, I coughed, almost spilling the remainder of my freegea on the table.

"Are you okay?" Melissa got up on her knees and smacked my back.

"Fine," I rasped after gaining my composure. "What made you think Garyck and I were together?"

"Because you can understand the funny noises he makes," she giggled, plopping back down on the bench. "And he always lets you take his arm band. He doesn't let anyone else do that."

Most people found Garyck intimidating, but the young ones never shied away from him. "We're not a couple. We're just friends." Saying it out loud saddened me more than I cared to admit.

I had a natural gift for obtaining items. Most people would call it stealing, but I preferred to think of it as procuring things without being caught. I didn't want to receive a lecture from my friends, so I let Melissa believe that Garyck let me take his band, when in truth, he never felt it leave his arm.

"Aren't you his,"—Melissa wrinkled her nose—"you know, that keti thing?"

"You mean ketiorra," I corrected.

"Yeah, that."

"Maybe Sloane is his ketiorra, and he's too scared to tell her," Laria said.

"Sure, that's it," I laughed. Nothing scared Garyck, or any of the vryndarr for that matter, and Laria knew it.

If Zaedon, Khyron, and Thrayn knew anything about the situation, they weren't talking. They seemed more than happy to let me handle any questions the child had about the bond between mates. I shot them each a narrow-eyed glare, promising that I'd get even later. Khyron didn't flinch. Thrayn lowered his gaze, seemingly fascinated with something on the floor. Zaedon's smile faded, and his tail twitched, gaining an amused grin from Cara.

"You know how Harper and Rygael have a special connection?" I asked.

"Uh-huh." Melissa bobbed her head. "Rygael did a lot of sniffing and knew Harper was his mate."

If Melissa knew that ketaurrans recognized their match

by scent, then explaining why Garyck and I weren't together might be easier than I'd expected. "That's right, but—"

"Garyck sniffs you all the time." The child crossed her arms, her gaze accusatory. "I've seen him."

I'd noticed too, but it didn't change anything. "Yes, and since he hasn't said anything, it probably means we're not meant for each other." I ignored the painful knot forming in my gut.

"Or maybe he needs to have one of your special talks, like the one you gave Khyron to help him win me over," Celeste said to Melissa.

My friend's circumstances had been different; a relationship with complications. "Or maybe everyone should mind their own business and leave it alone." I glared at Celeste, then smiled at Melissa and softened my voice. "I appreciate your concern, but giving Garyck one of your talks won't be necessary."

"Okay." Melissa didn't sound convinced, and I worried she might interfere anyway, especially if she received some nudging from Celeste and Laria.

Before I could insist the three of them remain neutral, Lily, one of three children Harper and Rygael had adopted while our group was dealing with mercenary issues in the city, opened the door. "There you are," she huffed at Melissa as she stomped into the room with a chonderra following close behind her.

The adorable creature was rare, their bodies covered in tufts of white fur and violet scales. He wasn't much bigger than a small Earth dog, which was why the children had turned him into a pet. "Fuzzball and I have been looking all over for you."

Melissa rolled her eyes and flashed Lily a where-else-would-I-be look, then stuck her hand under the table and let Fuzzball lick her with the forked end of his long orange tongue. Once he was done, he worked his way over to Celeste and snatched the small piece of pytienna, a flat cake made from plants, that she held out for him.

"Harper wants to know what you want to do about the dresses for your wedding," Lily said to Celeste.

"Nobody said anything about having to wear dresses," I snapped. The environment could be harsh, so most of the inhabitants wore pants. The last time I'd worn a skirt was when we were still traveling through space. I'd only done it because my father had insisted I look presentable for some event we were attending.

He'd been the only blood relative I'd had on the ship, and he'd lost his life during the war. Thinking about him brought back painful memories. I swallowed past the constriction building in my throat and pushed the unwanted thoughts aside by refocusing my energies on persuading Celeste to change her mind.

It would've been easier if she hadn't already convinced Laria to join her efforts. Normally, I supported Celeste's decisions and was thrilled to be a part of her upcoming nuptials. But I strongly detested wearing anything that didn't completely cover my legs, and my friends knew it, which is why they hadn't consulted me first.

Not one to give up until I'd exhausted all available resources, I turned to Khyron, hoping to gain an ally. "Don't the ketaurrans have their own requirements regarding ceremonial apparel?"

Always the diplomat, Khyron pondered my question before answering. "We have no official bonding ceremony. Our vows are made in private." The smile he gave Celeste held a wicked glint. I didn't need to ask what they'd been doing when they sealed their bond.

"I do not know what a human wedding entails, so I am leaving the planning to my ketiorra," he added. "I will support whatever Celeste wants."

Love shone in the look Khyron cast his mate, causing a jealous pang in my chest. I was happy for my friends, and though I would never admit it out loud, a part of me longed for the same thing.

"Good, then it's settled," Celeste said, clapping her hands. "Lily, please tell Harper we'll come by and get her when we're ready to take a trip to the traders market."

The market was comprised of vendors who traveled between the cities and settlements, either selling items they'd handcrafted, things they'd derived from plants or objects they'd procured from other places. I couldn't recall ever seeing any dresses on display, but that didn't mean Celeste wouldn't be able to find someone who could design what she was after.

"I will," Lily said, then turned to Melissa. "Harper said you're supposed to come home now. You too, Fuzzball." She made a clicking noise and patted her leg to get the animal to follow her.

"Okay," Melissa mumbled, then after reluctantly climbing off the bench. She leaned forward and wrapped her arms around my neck, then whispered in my ear, "Let me know if you change your mind and want me to help you with Garyck."

I admired her determination and tried not to smile. "I promise you'll be the first person I ask."

After flashing a huge grin, she hurried to catch up with Lily and Fuzzball, who were already on their way outside.

Burke, along with Ryan, one of the males who helped guard the rocky perimeter running along a portion of the settlement's border, filed into the room at the same time the girls were leaving.

"So, what's going on in here?" Burke asked, heading toward the counter running along the back wall. He held up a cup and pointed at the container of freegea, offering to pour Ryan something to drink as well.

"We were discussing the wedding and my plans for the dresses," Celeste said, smirking at me.

"You girls are going to dress up for the ceremony?" Burke asked as he strolled around the table, plopped into the chair at the end, then leaned back and propped his feet on the nearest bench. "Now that's something I can't wait to see."

"I wouldn't mind seeing that myself," Ryan said, glancing in my direction. "I take it you're one of the fortunate ones."

Unfortunate was more like it, but I didn't say it aloud.

The male had been flirting with me since he'd first arrived in the settlement, so I wasn't surprised when he walked past Burke, then sat in the seat Melissa had vacated.

"There will actually be five of us. I've also asked Harper to organize things and Cara to be in the wedding party," Celeste said.

"Shouldn't be a problem," Cara gave me a mischievous wink, knowing it annoyed me when she sided with our friends.

"Well, it's a problem for me," I said. "Where am I going to put my blades?"

Ryan grinned as he lowered his dark gaze to my chest. "I can think of—"

"If you value certain parts of your anatomy, you won't finish that sentence," I said, cutting him off and tapping the hilt of the blade attached to my hip.

Even with my back to the door, when it opened again, I didn't need to look or hear Celeste's greeting to know that Garyck had entered the room. I'd been able to sense his nearness from the first time we'd met.

For a big guy, the male possessed the stealth of a predatory animal, more so than the other vryndarr. He'd never been much of a conversationalist, so the grunt Celeste received wasn't unexpected. Nor was the fact that he planned to continue keeping his distance when he leaned against the wall next to Zaedon.

CHAPTER TWO

GARYCK

Now that my friends and I had returned to the settlement, I rose early every day to go hunting. Today, Burke, the male in charge of the place, had asked Jardun and me to accompany him on a tour of the community's perimeter to observe the males who patrolled the area.

We were vryndarr, elite warriors who protected the drezdarr and all the planet's inhabitants. We also had exceptional hunting and tracking skills, honed since we were young. With the possibility of war looming in our future, Burke had wanted our expertise to ensure the residents were well-protected.

The human males did a good job, but they were trained to protect, whereas Jardun and I were conditioned to notice anything out of the ordinary.

A few months ago, a group of luzardees, mercenaries with beady black eyes, flat faces, and tan skin that shed annually, had infiltrated the settlement. They attempted to end Khyron's life, so I understood Burke's concern for constant vigilance. I was happy to help prevent any future breaches from happening again.

Once we'd completed our task and provided Burke with suggestions, he'd offered Jardun and me a ride back to the headquarters building in his solarveyor. I declined, preferring to walk and take the shortcut through the bordering forest and the back side of town.

Obviously, so did Vince, another team member, because he'd trailed along beside me. I was not much of a conversationalist, something Vince was quite aware of but did not seem to mind. The male chatted the entire trip, discussing random topics, most of which were trivial.

Burke, Ryan, and Jardun must have stopped along the way because they reached the entrance when Vince and I walked around the corner of the building.

Unlike the city, where a majority of the buildings were handcrafted from stone, the dwellings in the settlement were constructed from wood. Heavy rainfall could be a problem, so most of the structures, including this one, had a covered platform extending around the entire exterior.

"Nice walk?" Jardun asked, stopping to wait for us.

"Not bad," Vince said. "Garyck's a great listener."

Jardun chuckled. "He is indeed."

Melissa, Lily, and their pet Fuzzball exited the building after Ryan and Burke went inside. Having the young ones visit our group was not uncommon, but the response I had intended to give my friend was not one they should overhear, so I refrained from sharing it.

"Morning," Jardun said to the young females.

"Good morning to you too," Lily said and kept walking.

Melissa stopped in the middle of the platform but didn't say anything. She acted as if she had something on her mind, something she was not happy about.

"Melissa, is something wrong?" Vince asked.

She ignored Vince, then crossed her arms and tipped her head back to glare at me. "I really like Sloane, and,"—she scrunched her face—"just so you know, I promised I wouldn't have the talk with you until she says it's okay."

Talk? Usually, the child was friendly toward me. I did not understand what I had done to earn her anger, but she rushed off to catch up with Lily before I could ask.

"What did you do to Sloane?" Vince asked after the two young females disappeared around the corner.

"I did not do anything to Sloane," I grumbled, ignoring the guilt associated with knowing that I should have. The urge to claim her as my ketiorra grew stronger with each passing day. Some days worse than others.

Vince stepped up on the porch. "Maybe that's the problem." He chuckled as he entered the building.

I had been working with the humans for a while now. Yet, at times, they were confusing, and I did not understand their humor. However, this time, I did not have a problem figuring out the sexual innuendo. Sharing my bed with the beautiful female had filled my thoughts from the first time I had inhaled her enticing scent.

I entered the building in time to hear Sloane threaten to remove Ryan's male parts, and for a moment, I thought about encouraging her. The teasing in her voice reminded me of the banter we used to share. Something that had not occurred in a long time, the blame belonging entirely to me.

Sloane was quick to mask the glimpse she had stolen of the band on my arm. It had become a playful game between us. One, it appeared, she missed as much as I did. It had been days since the last time she had removed it, and for some reason, the metal's weight seemed as heavy as my guilt.

My resolve to avoid Sloane started to slip, so I concentrated on the reasons for my recent decisions. The mental scars I retained after being tortured by Sarus's males were nothing compared to the shame I carried over the death of Khyron's sire. I remembered the horrific battle as if it had happened yesterday. Many had died, many had been injured, including Khyron. I had been taken prisoner, and if not for my friends, I would not have survived.

I had to stay focused on finding the missing weapons. Failing now would mean the loss of many lives, possibly even Sloane's. The thought of her no longer existing brought an unbearable ache to my chest. I had to be strong, to see our mission through to the end. Only then would I do whatever it took to claim the feisty female, to keep her by my side and in my bed.

Sloane was an experienced warrior. Though, at times, her boldness frustrated me. The females on our planet were not fighters. It was a male's duty to protect them. It took time to accept that some human females possessed the skills to defend themselves as well as others.

I was in awe every time I watched Sloane in action. She might be several inches shorter and smaller than her female friends, but it never hindered her abilities.

Even now, memories of her previous fights combined with being near the female had my body reacting, my shaft hardening. Thankfully, I had not removed my thigh-length jacket, which kept my discomfort from being noticed.

Instead of sitting at one of the empty places at the long rectangular table, I leaned against the wall next to Zaedon and his mate Cara. "Why are you standing over here?" I asked, keeping my voice low so the others could not hear me.

"Because I do not want to be sitting at the table when Cianna arrives," Zaedon said. "If she takes a place next to me, I will have to share my pytienna with her."

Everyone knew about his fondness for the flat cakes. "But you never share with anyone, not even your mate," I said, amused that Zaedon had pulled the container he held closer to his chest.

"I know, but she makes this face." Zaedon mimicked a pout. "And since she is going to have a young one, I am unable to say no."

I missed whatever had been said before Sloane pushed away from the table and got to her feet. "You guys decide what you want to do about the dresses, and let me know," she said. "Until then, I'm going to go workout."

"I'm free if you need someone to spar with and help you with that pent-up anxiety," Ryan said. "I'll even promise to go easy on you." He cracked his knuckles and winked at her.

Sloane rolled her eyes. "I don't have pent-up anxiety. And you're the one who should be asking me to take it easy on you."

Ryan's laughter grated. I did not like the male, nor did I trust him. He had arrived in the settlement when our team was still in the city, and Burke had put him to work guarding the perimeter. Burke was suspicious of all newcomers, and I was glad to learn he had assigned Vince to work with Ryan.

The way the male was constantly hanging around Sloane and flirting with her did not make me happy either. Working out with Sloane would include bodily contact. The thought of the male touching her in any way had me growling and inching away from the wall.

Zaedon grabbed my arm and kept me in place. "Did you seriously think she would wait for you forever?" he asked, using the same low voice that I had.

It seemed my actions had not gone unnoticed by the rest of the team. Had Ryan drawn the same assumptions? Was he paying extra attention to Sloane because he believed I no longer wanted her?

Cara leaned forward to see me around Zaedon. "Especially after the way you've been ignoring her lately." Her voice was low as well but laced with sarcasm.

She was not wrong, but I was not willing to discuss my behavior or the reason behind it. My snort was drowned out by the loud rumble of a solarveyor's engine approaching the building faster than necessary. The loud screech of the vehicle's brakes had Cara cringing. She was an expert when it came to anything mechanical and would know better than anyone else in the room if something was wrong with the transport.

The only vehicles allowed to park near the building were the ones that belonged to the people inside the room. We were all on edge, afraid an attack might come at any minute. None of us were inclined to relax until the missing laser weapons were found and destroyed. Anyone who carried a blade was instinctively reaching for their hips.

Cara was well-trained in combat and preferred to use her body as a weapon, so she did not carry any weapons like the rest of us. At least none that were visible. It was possible she had a dagger hidden in her boot.

She was also a fearless warrior and had the door open before Zaedon and I could reach it. Her mate growled her name, then muttered something about her independent stubbornness as he dropped the container on the floor. Zaedon might obsess about his favorite food, but he would give his life for Cara the same way I would give mine for Sloane.

Ketaurran males were raised to protect all females, our mates even more so. It had been difficult to accept that the human females who had been trained as warriors were capable of taking care of themselves and did not appreciate any male's interference.

The others in the room, those not already standing, were getting to their feet. I followed Zaedon to the door, my hand on the hilt of my blade, ready to assist if someone attacked his mate. I'd made it to the platform in time to see Cara jump to the ground and hurry toward the male exiting the vehicle.

He was tall with brownish blond hair, a darker shade covering his chin. As far as I was aware, the male was not a warrior, though the belt hanging low on his waist containing sheaths with short blades on each hip suggested otherwise.

"Des," Cara said, embracing him briefly. "I didn't think you ever left Golyndier."

The male grinned. "Normally, I don't travel far, but the

information I found for you was too important not to deliver in person."

"Welcome," Zaedon said to Des, then dismissed him to speak with Cara. "How did you know it was safe to open the door?" As the humans would say, my friend was more laid back than the rest of the vryndarr, yet his tone was laced with concern and irritation.

No one could blame him for being worried about his mate's safety. Not after learning that the missing laser blasters were in the hands of those who wanted to end Khyron's life and take control of the planet.

Stress had become a constant companion for all of us. Being armed with blades did not help morale when we knew a well-placed hit from one of the advanced weapons could end our lives.

"Because if I were going to attack someone, I wouldn't use a noisy vehicle that was about to break down," Cara said, then returned her attention to Des. "I'm surprised you made it this far."

Des shrugged, then chuckled. "Me too."

"Come on, we can worry about repairing it later," Cara said, heading back toward the building.

Realizing that there was no threat, everyone had returned to their seats or wherever they were standing when Cara led Des inside.

"Cara," Khyron said, clearing his throat. "Would you like to introduce us to your friend?"

"Sure," Cara said, smiling as she closed the door. "Everyone, this is Des." Starting with me, she worked her way around the room.

"And that is the drezdarr and his mate Celeste." Cara continued by pointing in Khyron's direction.

Des's eyes widened as he whispered, "Should I be bowing or something?"

"I would appreciate it if you did not," Khyron said. "And please call me Khyron." Besides being the drezdarr's protector, I was also his friend. He did not lead by flaunting his title or commanding respect. The trust he earned came naturally, derived from the honesty and integrity he bestowed upon others.

"Uh, okay, Khyron," Des said, his cheeks flushing.

Cara saved the male from further embarrassment by moving on to the next person. Sloane was sitting near the end of the table and was the last one to be introduced. "You're the one who makes all those beautiful knives and swords, aren't you?" she asked.

"You've seen my work?" Des asked.

"Yes, and please tell me you brought along some extras you'd be willing to part with."

"Sloane," Celeste said, shaking her head.

"What? A girl can never have too many blades."

"I believe we have more important things to discuss than adding to your arsenal," Laria said.

"Fine," Sloane groaned. To Des, she said, "We'll definitely talk later."

"Now that you've met everyone, do you want to tell us what you're doing here?" Cara asked, placing her hands on her hips. "And should I be worried about what a personal visit will cost me? I can't afford to buy your entire collection of blades."

From what Cara had shared with the group, her associate dealt with information. Des handcrafted exquisite knives, daggers, and swords. He required at least one of the items to be purchased before he shared what he knew.

"No charge," Des said, furrowing his brows. "I'm doing my part to prevent another war, which wouldn't be good for business, especially if I have to fight and don't survive."

"Great, so what did you find out?" Cara asked.

"Actually, not a lot," he grinned and held up a hand. "But I believe the male shackled in my vehicle has the information you're after."

Finding someone who could provide us with the answers we needed was not an easy task and earned Des my respect.

"You have our deepest thanks," Khyron said, pushing away from the table. "I am certain Burke and my vryndarr have many questions for the male. I would appreciate it if you accompanied us." Those of us who knew the drezdarr recognized his statement as an order, not a request. An order that meant the females needed to stay behind and keep Ryan away from the interrogation.

"Vince," Burke said. "Would you find Logan and let him know about our guests?"

When it came to extracting information, Logan was the most ruthless. Now that his mate Cianna was going to have a young one, he had no problem letting the others take over. Though, I suspected, he'd step in and help if Burke or Khyron asked him to.

"Not at all," Vince said. He didn't seem to mind not being invited to the interrogation, but judging by the scowls on the females's faces, they weren't happy about being excluded but would follow Khyron's request anyway.

CHAPTER THREE

GARYCK

It turned out that Everett, the male Des had shackled in his solarveyor, had worked for Doyle before his death. He was one of the mercs who had absconded with some of the laser blasters. Everett had made the mistake of trying to find a buyer for the weapons in Golyndier, which was how Des learned about him.

The information the male possessed was critical to our current mission and not something we wanted anyone outside of our team to overhear. Burke had suggested we relocate to a secure location, which happened to be the detainment room in a smaller structure located behind the main headquarters building.

Since Jardun, Zaedon, and I had accompanied Khyron and Burke, Thrayn stayed behind with Celeste. Thrayn took guarding the mated couple seriously and refused to leave either of them without additional protection.

Thrayn might be the latest to join the vryndarrs, but he'd proven himself to be a good warrior. Watching him interact with the human females, specifically those who could fight, had been interesting. Not that dealing with their independent nature had been an easy adjustment for any of us.

Burke had a military background and had worked security on the spaceship before the crash. I had witnessed his interrogation techniques on other occasions. He was an expert at extracting information and did not usually require assistance. Hearing what Everett had to say should have been a priority, but I couldn't stop thinking about Sloane.

It was difficult to focus on the conversation around me, or reign in my frustration, knowing that she was probably working out in the training room with Ryan. They would be practicing hand-to-hand maneuvers, and the male would touching her body.

It was a good thing Khyron had requested my presence; otherwise, I would have tracked the male down and delivered several well-placed punches.

I fisted my fingers, annoyed that my thoughts had my tail swishing. The movement did not go unnoticed by Zaedon, who was leaning against the wall next to me. He raised a curious brow. "Are you anxious for the bloodletting to begin, or are you thinking about a certain blue-eyed female?"

I snorted. "You should mind your own business."

"Aww, the female then," he chuckled.

"You can't do this." Everett's ranting drew my attention and ended the urge to wipe the smug grin off Zaedon's face. He sat in a chair in the middle of the room, his hands secured behind his back, his ankles strapped to the chair legs. Burke and Jardun had made sure he was not going anywhere, no matter how much he exerted himself.

And, at the moment, he was fighting the bindings a lot.

"I'm pretty sure they can," Des said, striding toward the door. "It looks like you have everything under control, so I'll be in the gathering room if you need me."

"With all the weapons you make, I never would've guessed you were squeamish," Burke teased.

"Oh, I'm not. Interrogations just aren't my thing." Des

grinned and raised a brow at Everett. "And neither is the mess they make."

Everett frantically tugged against his bonds. "You're not seriously going to leave me to be tortured by these *lizards*, are you?"

My friends and I ignored the male's insult. It was not the first time we had been compared to a lower life-form from Earth, nor would it be the last. I found it amusing that he thought insulting us would help his cause. Unfortunately, he was mistaken. Burke was not as forgiving as we were. The disapproving glare he gave Everett promised retribution for the remark on our behalf.

Everett swallowed hard. Perspiration appeared on his forehead. Both signs that he was more afraid than he wanted us to believe.

"As a matter of fact…yeah," Des said, opening the door. "I'd suggest you answer their questions, and truthfully; otherwise, your blood will be joining the stains on the floor."

Everett jerked his gaze to the area around his chair and groaned. The few times I'd been in the room, I had not paid attention to the darkened spots in the wood, of which there were many.

Des's laughter slowly faded as he walked away from the building.

"I like Cara's friend," Jardun said. "As Laria would say, he has a maniacal dark side."

Des was a likable male, and I grunted my agreement.

Burke took an intimidating step toward Everett. "I understand that you know where we can find the laser blasters you helped Doyle recover from the *Starward Bounty*."

I hoped the interrogation proved useful, and we obtained the location of the weapons. I also could not wait for the questioning to be over. Not because I could not handle seeing what was about to happen. I had seen a lot worse during the war. I was anxious to see Sloane, even from a distance, and considered getting closer under the guise of perusing Des's weapons.

"I don't know anything about that, no matter what he says," Everett said, glaring at the closed door. "I was in the traders market getting supplies and minding my own business when your friend jumped me and brought me here."

Burke cracked his knuckles. "Since you have an aversion to lizards, maybe we should dump you in one of the ravines and see how you do with the leezacorr."

The small cave-dwelling creatures had black scaly skin and translucent green eyes. They might prefer dark places and avoid people, but it did mean they were not dangerous. And in some circumstances, deadly. Judging by the widening of Everett's eyes, he was familiar with the leezacorrs.

"That is not a bad idea," Khyron said.

"Do you want to go on foot through the forest?" Jardun asked. He placed a hand on Everett's wrist and withdrew his blade, acting as if he was going to free the male.

"No, we can get there faster if we take a solarveyor," Khyron said, his tone convincing.

None of us had addressed Khyron by his title. Everett must have known him by sight and realized that any order he gave would be carried out without question. It seemed facing an excruciating death over torture was Everett's breaking point. His face paled, and he muttered, "My friends and I are keeping the blasters at an outpost near the Quaddrien."

"And the rest of the weapons?" Burke asked. "I need the name of the male who purchased them from Doyle."

We knew a ketaurran male was involved because Cara had seen one of the weapons hidden inside his jacket the night she and Logan confronted Doyle. No one knew the identity of the male. He had disappeared, and though we had done an extensive search, we had yet to find him.

"I don't know," Everett said.

"Why should we believe you?" Burke clenched his fist.

"Doyle never told me," Everett said, wincing. "I swear."

"I have a feeling he might be telling the truth." Jardun backed away and returned his blade to its sheath.

"I am," Everett said.

"For your sake, I hope so," Zaedon said, then clapped my shoulder. "It has been quite some time since my friend here has used a human as bait when hunting."

There were times when I did not find Zaedon's humor amusing, but this was not one of them.

CHAPTER FOUR

SLOANE

It had been weeks since Khyron sent Cara and Zaedon to meet with Des and ask him to discreetly see what he could learn about the missing laser blasters. I didn't think anyone in the room actually believed Des would find out anything new, let alone show up at the settlement in person. Or produce a male with critical information.

My friends and I had tangled with Doyle and some of his males on several occasions, the last time being the same night he'd ended up dead. I'd never met Everett before he'd arrived with Des. We avoided the mercs because they had bad reputations and didn't have a problem expressing themselves with their fists or blades. Taking lives to get what they wanted was also on their list of transgressions.

I knew via Cara that Des was a craftsman and great at providing information. She'd never said anything about him doing any fighting, so I was surprised to see the short swords sheathed to his hips. I had a feeling the weapons weren't just for show, that Des knew how to use them. It would explain how he'd managed to secure Everett. Height-wise, the males were close to six feet tall, but

Everett had a brawnier frame and easily outweighed Des by ten pounds.

I tipped my head from side to side, stretching my neck muscles. I would rather be in the detainment room with the males observing the interrogation instead of working out with Ryan. Khyron wouldn't have purposely omitted Laria, Celeste, and me if he hadn't expected us to keep an eye on Ryan. Since the male's interest in me was obvious, I'd been selected as the unlucky person to keep him occupied.

Ryan's idea of a hand-to-hand battle included more groping than necessary. If I thought it would do any good, I'd kick him between the legs and make it look like an accident.

I knew how to defend myself, and it irked me that he was holding back because I was a female, which was why I used all my strength when my elbow connected with his ribs. If nothing else, he'd learn not to underestimate my skills. Skills I'd learned from Logan, one of the best human fighters on our team.

He was Burke's second-in-command and also in charge of training. He'd taught my friends and me everything he knew about fighting. He'd never held back during any of our sessions. Logan told us the enemy wouldn't have any mercy and taught us how to defend ourselves against all possible attacks.

Cara had gotten so good at using her body as a weapon that she refused to carry a blade. At least none that were visible. I was sure she kept a dagger hidden in her boot just like Laria, Celeste, and I did. The three of us preferred using blades, but when it came to wielding knives, Celeste never missed.

"Damn, Sloane. Is wearing a dress really that bad?" Ryan asked, rubbing his side.

I was okay with letting Ryan believe the frustration I was working off had to do with Celeste's announcement about her wedding. In truth, I was annoyed with myself for caring about Garyck.

"You can always take my place," I said. "I'll bet you'd look good in ruffles. Maybe a pretty shade of pink." Since our arrival on the planet, I hadn't seen any clothing made from bright colors, nor did I think it was possible. Most outfits were varying shades of black and brown, sometimes gray. They were designed for the harsh environment, not to make a fashion statement.

It might not be the smartest thing, but I couldn't resist goading males with large egos. And Ryan's was exceedingly huge. During our training sessions, Logan made sure we knew how important it was not to lose control or announce our attacks.

It was too bad Ryan had never been given the same advice. He had a habit of letting his emotions control his movements, evidenced by the growl he released before lunging and giving me the advantage. I spun out of his reach, then shoved him with my foot. He lost his balance and ended up on his hands and knees.

"Nice move," he said through gritted teeth as he pushed off the mat, then turned to face me. I braced for retaliation, welcomed it even. Instead, Ryan took a deep breath and flexed his fingers to regain composure.

He leaned forward, arms outstretched as he sidestepped, looking for an opening to come at me again. "What do you think is going on out back?"

"Don't know. Don't care," I said, shrugging. Ryan clearly had an agenda. No surprise there. We were all suspicious of his timely arrival in the settlement and his interest in what my friends were doing.

The additional attention he paid me hadn't gone unnoticed by Burke. With Garyck keeping his distance, Burke made the same assumptions I had and hadn't hesitated to exploit the situation. I'd balked when he'd first asked me to get closer to Ryan.

Underneath his dangerous persona, Burke was a decent male. But when it came to saving lives, specifically the humans, he could be ruthless. It only took a little reminder about what was at stake for everyone I cared about for me to agree to help him. He'd also asked me to keep what I was doing between the two of us until it became necessary to tell the others.

Burke hadn't asked, nor did I believe he ever would, but I'd made it very clear that I wouldn't ask Ryan to share my bed or join him in his. I couldn't see the harm in doing some flirting if it got the male to let down his guard so I could gain some much-needed information.

"Come on, Sloane," Ryan said, continuing to circle to my right. "Aren't you a little curious to know why Khyron and the other males are being so secretive and why they didn't invite you along?"

I already knew Ryan was the reason my friends and I had been left behind, but I wasn't about to tell him that. "Maybe, but I'm sure if the drezdarr wants us to know what he's doing, he'll tell us."

This time when Ryan reached for me, I grabbed his arm and dropped, tucking my legs as I went. I pressed my feet against his midsection, using the momentum to propel him forward, so he landed on his back.

A satisfied smirk tugged at my lips when I heard Ryan hit hard and groan. The covering on the floor didn't provide any cushioning, and he'd be feeling the jolt for at least a day, maybe longer. I quickly rolled away and sprung to my feet, keeping plenty of distance between us.

"I'd say the match goes to Sloane." I heard Des's voice and glanced toward the doorway where he leaned against the frame, sipping from a tall mug filled with a dark amber liquid.

"Nayea told me where to find you," Des said.

Nayea was an older ketaurran female and also the resident doctor. Besides looking after the males who resided in the headquarters building, she made one heck of an ale. I tipped my head toward Des's drink. "It looks like that's not the only thing Nayea helped you find."

Des chuckled, then held up his drink as if offering a toast. "If I were looking for a new place to live, this would be a great motivator."

"I'll be the first to admit that Nayea's ale is the best I've ever tasted," Ryan said. He hadn't moved from the mat. I thought about offering my hand to help him up, but I'd had enough bodily contact with the male to last me for quite some time.

"What do you say we call it quits for today?" I asked.

"Only if you agree to a rematch," Ryan said, slowly pushing to his feet.

"Sure." I grabbed a couple of towels off a nearby stack and tossed one at him, then walked over to stand next to Des.

Ryan took his time leaving, as if lingering would gain him the information he wanted. He finally gave up and left when the silence between us became uncomfortable. I waited until his footsteps in the hallway faded before saying anything to Des. "Any news?" I asked.

"Not that I'm aware of," he said. "I left before they got started." He took another sip. "Are you still interested in looking at some of my blades?"

"Absolutely." I grinned. "Just give me a few minutes to get cleaned up."

CHAPTER FIVE

SLOANE

Des was truly a gifted craftsman. Still unable to believe my luck at obtaining the treasure, I admired the knife and sighed as I caressed the smooth blue-black finish with my fingertip.

The ore used to craft the blade was rare, highly coveted, and made great weapons. The few I'd handled had excellent precision when throwing. Even someone with adequate skills could generally hit their targets.

I sat on one end of the lounger in the lower level gathering room of the dwelling I shared with Celeste, Laria, and their mates while I waited for the other members of the team to arrive. The headquarters building was open to anyone in the settlement. Rather than have someone stand guard outside to keep people out and possibly draw unwanted attention, Burke and Khyron had decided to hold the meeting at our place.

Now that Jardun and Khyron lived with us, I sometimes felt out of place. I was happy my friends had found their mates, yet envied them at the same time.

I was curious to hear what the males had learned

during Everett's interrogation. I'd expected the questioning to last several hours and was surprised when it didn't. Everett must not have been as tough as he appeared. Either that or Burke was getting better at extracting information.

With any luck, whatever the males learned would be useful, and we'd be heading out soon to find and destroy the laser blasters Doyle's males had kept for themselves.

It was possible Everett also knew the location of the mysterious ketaurran and where he'd taken the other weapons, but I wasn't too hopeful. In my experience, things were never that easy.

When my thoughts started drifting in Garyck's direction, I got up and paced the floor. Now was not the time to ponder what might have been if I'd actually been his ketiorra. The upcoming mission was too important. Lives were at stake, and I needed to stay focused.

Laria was the first to saunter into the room, her gaze drawn to my new blade. "Did you get that from Des?" I could hear the appreciation in her voice and held it out for her inspection.

"Yeah. Beautiful, isn't it?" I asked.

"It's a true work of art," Laria said, then handed it back to me.

Celeste walked into the room next. "We might need to check out the rest of Des's collection before he leaves."

My friends valued a good blade as much as I did. Des would most likely head back to Golyndier with quite a few more cradassons than he'd arrived with.

I heard the main door open, followed by the sound of numerous footsteps as more of the group headed our way. Since the other team members had already been invited, no one bothered to knock before entering.

After returning the blade to the sheath on my hip, I sat back down on the lounger and shifted sideways to see who else had arrived. Khyron, Jardun, and Thrayn led the way, followed by Burke, Zaedon, Cara, and Des.

A few minutes later, Vurell, the drezdarr's physician, walked into the room. "Hey, Doc," I said, surprised to see him make an appearance. Lately, he'd been keeping to himself. I missed his overbearing presence and sense of humor. Most of all, I hated seeing him in such a depressed state. Even though we'd finally found the traitor who'd poisoned Khyron and nearly ended his life, I knew Vurell had taken what happened personally.

Just because the male had worked closely with Vurell, it didn't make him responsible. It was hard to get rid of guilt. It might diminish with each passing day, but it never went away, not entirely.

Hopefully, with a little time, Vurell would be able to move past it. On the upside, Khyron's near-death experience had been the catalyst that had pulled us all together, that and his collaboration to unite all the planet's inhabitants.

"Sloane," Vurell said, acknowledging me with a nod before finding a place on the opposite side of the room.

Garyck was the last to arrive. His intense amber gaze locked with mine before he found a spot near the wall and close to the entryway. It didn't matter where we had our meetings. He was always diligent about guarding an access point.

My stomach fluttered the way it always did at the sight of him, and I forced myself to look away.

Laria went to stand beside Jardun, and Celeste and Khyron took a seat on the lounger next to me. Burke stood in the center of the room, arms crossed facing the rest of us. "You'll all be happy to know that Everett told us the blasters Doyle kept for himself are being stored in an outpost near the Quaddrien."

"Finally, something promising," I muttered. The news was the best thing I'd heard all day and seemed to magically lift the melancholy that had been clinging to our group for weeks.

My friends and I had been to an outpost in that area

before. I wasn't thrilled about the location, but I was glad we finally had one.

"Did he know anything about our mysterious friend," Cara asked.

"No, and I got the impression he didn't want to know. Not after what happened to Doyle," Burke said.

"So, what's the plan then?" Laria asked.

"We need to—" Burke didn't get to finish because a loud rap on the main door drew everyone's attention. Vince didn't wait for anyone to answer. He stumbled into the room, supporting Marcus, who was clutching a wound on the side of his head. Marcus's movements were sluggish, a sign that the blow he'd received had been substantial.

"Sorry to interrupt, but I couldn't find Nayea," Vince scanned the group until he saw Vurell. "Marcus needs your help."

"What happened?" Khyron growled, pushing off the lounger, then helping Vince get Marcus settled into his seat.

"I went to take the prisoner a meal and found him like this," Vince said.

Seeing Marcus's injury must have jolted something inside Vurell. Within seconds, he'd snapped back into physician mode. "Let me see." He urged Marcus to lower his blood-covered hand.

I scooted forward so I could see around Celeste. The gash looked nasty and was still bleeding. Vurell always traveled with his medical kit when he left the city, and I assumed he'd left it in his room in the headquarters building. Rather than run and retrieve it, I asked, "What do you need?"

"Water and something to clean the wound," Vurell said. "Healing salve, if you have any."

"What about some creevea?" Jardun asked, pulling a small pouch out of his pocket and handing it to Laria.

"Yes," Vurell said without looking. "It will help."

When brewed, the creevea plant produced an ugly yellow liquid that tasted awful but provided a natural stimulant with excellent healing properties. I'd never known the vryndarr to travel anywhere without some of the dried leaves.

It didn't take me long to gather the supplies Vurell needed. He had finished applying the salve by the time Laria returned. "Here." She handed a steaming mug to Marcus. "Be careful. It might be a little hot."

Marcus blew on the contents for a few seconds, then wrinkled his nose as he took a sip.

Khyron patiently waited for Marcus to down several swallows before asking, "Can you tell us who did this to you?"

"It was Ryan," Marcus said, his angered voice raspy.

"And Everett?" Burke asked.

"Gone," Vince said. "I'm assuming Ryan took him." He glanced at Des. "Sorry, but I think he also stole your vehicle."

The fact that Vince hadn't found a body meant that Everett had been smart enough not to share the location of the weapons, forcing Ryan to take the male with him. Everett might be alive for now, but I had a feeling that would change once they reached the outpost and Ryan got what he was after.

Ryan was probably aware that we also had the location. The problem we faced now was whether or not we could get there ahead of the treacherous male. If Ryan was working with the mysterious ketaurran, as we'd suspected, then he needed to be stopped before he got his hands on the weapons and delivered them to our enemy.

"We need to prepare and leave immediately," Khyron said.

Normally, he was good at hiding his emotions in dire situations, but I glimpsed his concern before he masked his expression.

The moment we'd all been dreading had finally arrived.

There was a chance our attempts to confiscate the deadly laser weapons could cost one or more of us our lives. The decisions he was about to make had to be weighing on him heavily. Celeste placed a comforting hand on Khyron's arm as if she knew what he was thinking.

"We might still have an advantage," Des said.

"How so?" Burke asked.

"If Ryan took my transport, it will take him longer than normal to get anywhere. The thing moves okay but rarely reaches optimal speed."

I wanted to shake my head. How could someone who made such beautiful blades not put the same effort into their vehicle? Maybe we'd get lucky, and the darned thing would die on the road long before Ryan and Everett reached the outpost.

"How did they get inside your vehicle?" Cara asked. "Don't you have any security on the access door?" The situation was distressing the mechanic in her.

She'd made sure that the handful of solarveyors we used all had security, and only the immediate members of the team knew the codes. Not even the males who guarded the perimeter could use a vehicle without getting permission from Burke first.

"Sort of, but if someone wanted to get in, I suppose they could jimmy it with a knife," Des said. "And before you ask, the answer is "yes," the solars were charging so Ryan would have enough power to make it to the outpost."

There was no use getting angry with Des. If Ryan was determined to leave unnoticed, then he already had a backup plan. When he'd first shown up at the settlement, he'd given Burke a down-on-his-luck story, telling him he'd gotten a ride with a vendor from the traders market.

The market was on the other side of town. Alone, Ryan could have made it unnoticed. Dragging Everett along, if he'd been unwilling, would've drawn unwanted attention, and given us time to catch up with him. Des's vehicle had been convenient and helped with a quick escape.

According to Des, Everett had gone to Golyndier to obtain supplies by himself. There was no way he'd been working alone when he confiscated the laser blasters. "Did Everett tell you how many people were left guarding the weapons?"

"Yes," Burke said. "There are two other males."

"Decent odds then," Celeste said.

"I agree, but I don't think you and Khyron should be coming along," Burke said. "Or Jardun and Laria, for that matter."

"What?" Celeste slapped her hands on her hips. "Why not?"

Khyron didn't seem surprised by the announcement, which meant he'd already discussed the situation with Burke prior to the meeting.

"Ketaurrios needs strong leaders. We can't risk something happening to either of you," Burke said, his gaze never leaving Celeste.

Khyron took Celeste's hands in his. "As much as I would like to make the trip, I agree with Burke's assessment. We cannot leave the settlement unguarded."

"I understand the need for you to stay behind, but what about Jardun and me?" Laria didn't sound happy about the decision either.

Jardun pulled Laria into his arms. "I am the vryndarr leader. I have a sworn duty to remain with the drezdarr and drezdarrina." He softened his tone. "And as my mate, I hope you will agree to stay with me, fight by my side, if necessary."

I stifled a snort. When Jardun and Laria first met, things between them hadn't gone smoothly. It took time for him to realize she could take care of herself and wouldn't tolerate being offered his protection.

"Of course." Laria glanced around the room, frowning. "Then who gets to go?"

"Burke will be leading the mission," Khyron said.

"Anyone else who chooses to accompany him will be on a voluntary basis."

"Jardun will need my help, so I will remain with the drezdarr," Thrayn said.

We all had a score to settle with Ryan, but I was the one he'd targeted, hoping to extract information. "I'll go," I said, walking over and standing next to Burke.

"Sloane, you can't," Celeste said.

"I agree," Laria said.

I understood their trepidation. We'd always done everything together, worked as a team. "I need to do this," I said, hoping they'd understand without asking me to explain in front of everyone.

"Don't worry, Zaedon and I will look after her," Cara said, trying to reassure Laria and Celeste.

"Seriously," I huffed.

"Oh, I wasn't worried about you." Cara joined me, then nudged my arm. "I was more concerned about what you'd do to the other males when we finally catch up with them, specifically Ryan."

"I will go as well," Garyck said.

My jaw dropped, and I gaped at the male who'd been avoiding me for days. I thought for sure if I was going that he'd stay behind. We'd been on dangerous missions before, but never against anyone with superior weapons.

"Thank you all," Kyron said. He tipped his head and forced an appreciative smile to keep us from seeing how troubled he was at knowing that some of us might not survive.

"I'd like to tag along as well," Des said.

"It is not required," Khyron said. "You have done more than enough to help, for which we are all grateful."

"This is personal. If Everett tells anyone that I'm responsible for bringing him here, gathering intel will be impossible." Des grinned. "My solarveyor might be a piece of junk, but it's mine, and I want it back."

"Fair enough," Khyron said.

"Those of you who are coming with me, pack what you need and meet me at the headquarters building," Burke said. "We leave in half an hour."

Laria and Celeste hung back, cornering me after everyone else left the dwelling.

"You don't need to go," Celeste said. "The guys can handle this."

"You both have mates, and you need to stay with them." I wasn't looking for pity and held up my hand before either of them could say anything. "Besides, I have special talents that might come in handy."

Celeste shared a concerned glance with Laria, then said, "Fine, but I want you to promise me you'll be careful, and you'll be back in time for my wedding."

"I promise," I said, pulling both of them into a group hug, then heading for stairs to the upper level. I had no idea what our team was about to face and didn't want to go without grabbing more weapons and a change of clothes.

"Oh, and Sloane," Celeste said when I was halfway to the top.

I stopped with my hand on the rail. "Yeah."

"Don't think by going that you're getting out of wearing a dress," she said. "I know what size you wear."

I groaned and continued my ascent. I loved my friends dearly, but sometimes they could be extremely annoying.

CHAPTER SIX

GARYCK

The transport vibrated, swayed, and dipped to the side each time Cara drove over a worn and uneven area of the road. Usually, I would have taken control of the vehicle, but I was too distracted and angry at Sloane for volunteering for this mission. When Burke had announced that Celeste and Laria would not be going, I assumed Sloane would be staying behind as well.

I should have known better. The infuriating female was unpredictable and always doing the unexpected. The first time we met, Zaedon had informed her that I did not like being touched by others, a remnant from my days of being tortured by Sarus's followers. She had dismissed his warning, then boldly squeezed the muscle of my arm before returning the band she had stolen. It still amazed me how easily she could remove the metal strip without being noticed.

Sloane had taken a seat next to Burke on the bench that ran along the interior wall behind Cara. I stood opposite them, gripping the framework near the access door, trying not to let her presence distract me from our mission—a difficult task when every breath I took was filled with her enticing scent.

Since Ryan's arrival in the settlement, none of us had seen him interacting with anyone outside the people living in the headquarters building. It did not mean he was working alone.

He was an intelligent male and would know we had extracted the location of the weapons from Everett. He would also know that we would go after them once we found Marcus. If there were others, we faced the possibility that Ryan might have them attempt to stop us.

The towering rock formations provided the perfect place for an ambush. Tension thrummed through my system, and I fought to keep my gaze focused on the viewing pane and the surrounding landscape rather than Sloane.

It had been a tough choice, but Burke and Khyron had decided to keep our suspicions about Ryan's real purpose for showing up in our community limited to our small group. Not everyone who lived in the area could be trusted with the information.

Neither of them could have foreseen how Des's arrival with Everett would impact their decision. It was obvious Ryan had not cared if Marcus survived his injury. I was convinced that he knew the location of the mysterious ketaurran and the rest of the laser blasters. When we found Ryan, I planned to make him share the information and pay for his transgressions.

Zaedon was sitting in the co-pilot seat, his shoulders rigid, also scanning the area for any potential threats. The terrain gradually changed from sand-packed dirt to rock formations, which turned into high ledges on both sides of the vehicle. The road was wide enough to accommodate the transport, but our view of anything ahead was limited.

"Do you think it's possible we got ahead of Ryan?" Cara asked the group.

It was something to consider since the ground we

traveled was hard and left no visible traces of another vehicle, making tracking almost impossible.

"He had a good head start, so I doubt it," Burke said.

"If that's the case, we can always take a shortcut to catch up with him," Des said. He'd been casually stretched out on a bench behind me. After getting to his feet, he moved to stand between Cara and Zaedon.

"A shortcut would be nice, but unless you can make this baby climb rocks or fly,"—Cara gave the control console an affectionate pat—"then we're stuck to using this road."

"No flying, but there is another way," Des said, leaning forward to get a better view outside. "It's hard to spot, but there's a narrow road not far from here that will take us to the ridge overlooking the outpost."

If we continued on our current route, our transport would be visible long before we reached the outpost. And if the mercs had armed themselves with laser blasters, we would not be able to get close enough to stop them.

"And you know this how?" Cara shot a skeptical glance over her shoulder at Des, then slowed the vehicle.

Des grinned. "I wasn't always in the information business. I did other things during the war and got around quite a bit."

I was curious to know what those other things were but wasn't about to pry. We all had secrets, and I figured he would tell us if he wanted us to know his.

"There," Des pointed at an opening between two smooth rock walls.

Cara stopped. "Are you sure we'll fit?"

Des chuckled and patted her on the shoulder. "Depends on how good a driver you are."

"Des," Zaedon warned.

"I'm kidding." Des held up his hands. "We'll fit. Don't worry."

Between the accuracy of Des's statement and Cara's skills, we made it through the narrow winding passage unscathed. There were several points where the rock walls came within inches of the vehicle, and I was certain we would get wedged and trapped inside the transport.

Unfortunately, when the road widened and ended, we were boxed in with barely enough room to turn around. "Des," I growled. "Please explain how this is a shortcut."

My intimidating glare did not seem to bother the male. "Sorry, did I forget to mention that we'll also need to do some climbing?"

CHAPTER SEVEN

SLOANE

"Seriously, Des," I said. "This is your shortcut." I held a hand over my eyes to block out the sun as I gazed upward along the rocky slope, noting how far it was to the top of the ridge.

"It's not as bad as it looks," Des chuckled.

"No, it's worse," Cara said, sealing the transport's access door.

I slung the strap from my bag across my chest to leave my hands free and hopefully make climbing easier. The bag was heavy, the additional weight pressing on my back.

Since I had no idea how dangerous things might get once we reached the outpost, I wasn't about to leave any of the weapons I'd packed behind. Everyone else in the group must have been thinking the same thing because their bags appeared to be as bulky as mine.

Des led the way, and I got in line after Burke. When I was halfway to the top, my hands were covered with scrapes, and my arm and leg muscles ached. My shoulder near the base of my neck was sore from the strap digging into my skin. Other than occasionally losing my footing and dealing with backsliding after gripping loose rocks, the climb hadn't been too difficult.

"This would've been a lot faster if there'd been a herd of chaugwai nearby," I said. My friends and I had used them the last time we'd been in a similar rock-climbing situation. The creatures, who could scale rock walls, reminded me of large iguanas who were easily enticed with berries and could be ridden like horses.

"Are you saying you would like to be carried to the top, little one?" Garyck asked, his deep voice teasing.

I'd been so focused on making the journey without falling that I hadn't realized he was climbing right behind me. I ignored the flutter in my stomach, then stopped to glare back at him. "Why, are you offering?"

To everyone else, his grunts were only sounds, but I had no problem interpreting their meaning. The current noise sounded like a maybe, which I answered with a snort to let him know I didn't need his help, then resumed climbing. Though his laughter was unexpected, I knew he understood my message.

"Am I missing something here?" Des asked, confused.

"Nope," Cara said. "They've got a thing. It's hard to explain, but you get used to it after a while."

Once we reached the flattened top of the rock formation, Des glanced around and scratched the stubble on his chin. "If I remember right, the outpost is over there on the other side." He tipped his head to the left.

"Des, I swear if you got us lost…" Cara fumed.

"Hey, it's been a couple of years since I was here." Des was pretty agile for a big guy and didn't hesitate to put some distance between himself and Cara.

He crouched to stay out of sight as he neared the row of boulders sitting along the edge of the drop-off on the other side. "Ha, I was right," he said after leaning forward to peer below.

"You are fortunate, my friend," Zaedon said, clapping Des on the back. "My mate is very skilled at inflicting damage."

"And she has no problem providing a demonstration," Cara said, still irritated with Des.

"Point taken." He grinned. "It's not wise to upset the female warrior."

I cleared my throat and pressed my lips into a thin line.

"Correction," Des said. "All female warriors."

"I knew you were a smart male," I said, shooting a sidelong glance at Garyck. After the rest of us joined Des, I removed my bag and dropped it near my feet.

"Burke, did you remember to bring your binoculars," Cara asked.

"Of course," he smirked.

"You have binoculars...from Earth?" Des widened his eyes as soon as Burke removed them from his bag. "Do you know how rare these are?"

"I do," Burke said. "And if they should mysteriously disappear, someone will lose several fingers."

Des scowled. "Has anyone ever pointed out how bloodthirsty you all are?"

"Not recently," I laughed.

Burke used the binoculars to check the area below. "I see one solarveyor next to the nearest building and one male standing outside, possibly posted as a guard. I don't see any movement near the other two structures, so if Everett was telling the truth, and there are others, they're most likely inside."

"Do you hear that?" Zaedon asked. The ketaurrans had enhanced senses and detected sounds and smells long before humans could. I strained to listen, and it didn't take long before I heard the rumble of an engine.

Cara snatched the binoculars away from Burke and aimed them in the direction of the noise. "That has to be Des's solarveyor."

I squinted, but the dark spot moving in our direction was too far away and still blurry. "How can you tell?"

"By the unusual sounds the engine is making," Cara

said.

"Oh, yeah," I said when the transport got closer, and I could hear uneven hums and clinking. Des had been right about his transport's speed. The vehicle kept a steady pace but took longer than normal to reach the outpost.

Once the vehicle stopped, Burke picked up the binoculars again to get a better look. "I see Everett and Ryan, but it looks like they stopped to pick up a friend." He handed the binoculars to Cara. "Tell me if that's the male you saw with Doyle."

Cara aimed the eyeglasses. "Well, I'll be darned. That's him all right." She lowered the glasses. "It's nice to know we were right about Ryan."

"Can you tell if any of them are carrying blasters?" Zaedon asked.

Cara held up the binoculars again. "Everett and Ryan only have blades, but our *friend* is wearing a jacket, and the last time we met, he kept his weapon hidden, or at least tried to." She continued to watch. "It looks like they're all going inside."

We'd been searching for the male for weeks without any luck. It was great to have our suspicions confirmed, but the male's arrival changed things. I smiled, a plan formulating in my mind. "If Mr. Mysterious is here, he's after the weapons and will undoubtedly take them to the same location as the others he already got from Doyle. This could be the only chance we get to track them."

"What did you have in mind?" Burke asked.

I took a deep breath, gathering my thoughts before explaining the details of my plan to my friends. "I'm guessing the weapons containers are either in the building or the solarveyor we spotted when we arrived. If they're inside the building, I doubt Ryan and his friend will transfer them into Des's vehicle. We have to assume that they know we'll be looking for them and want to use the faster vehicle."

I paused, giving them time to ponder what I'd said so

far. When no one asked any questions, I continued. "I know obtaining these weapons is our first priority, but what if someone were to stow away on the solarveyor and let Ryan and his friend lead us to the other missing weapons?"

"What you're suggesting could be a death sentence for whoever goes if they get caught," Des said.

"I know," I said, glancing at Burke. He was the one person in the group I could count on to reasonably evaluate the merits of a suggestion without involving emotion. He furrowed his brows, and I knew he was calculating the odds of letting someone do what I'd suggested. "Let's say we decide to go ahead with your plan. We can't follow the transport without being seen. How do you propose we track them?"

I retrieved a hand-sized bag of zapharite stones out of my travel bag. The stones absorbed the sun's rays and gave off a blue-green glow, enough to light up small areas. They worked as well as any flashlight or candle back on Earth. Since I never knew where we'd end up spending our nights, I always kept a handful of the rocks with me.

What I was about to do was dangerous, but I had the new blade I'd gotten from Des sheathed to my hip and a thin dagger hidden in one of my boots. Though I was more than prepared for any situation, I gave my bag of weapons a regretful glance, hoping my friends would take care of them after I was gone.

"I'll leave a trail of rock crumbs for you to follow," I said, then slipped past the nearest boulder and over the rock's edge before anyone could disagree or try to stop me.

***

GARYCK

I did not understand Sloane's reference to rock crumbs. Not that it mattered, because I was too busy growling as I watched her move past the boulders we were using for cover and disappear over the rocky ledge heading for the outpost below.

I heard Zaedon mumble a ketaurran curse, and Cara call out, "Sloane, wait." Des seemed too astonished to speak. Burke gazed at the spot where Sloane had departed with a concerned, yet approving, expression, which had me fisting my hands and struggling not to throttle him.

"What does she think she is doing?" The words rushed out even though I already knew the answer. No one answered. Those of us close to her had surmised that Sloane had not been looking for volunteers when she shared her idea with us. She had already planned to be the one stowing away on the solarveyor.

After my attempt at teasing her during the climb, I knew she was upset with me. Normally, our playful banter did not include additional sarcasm or angered glares. Had my behavior over the last few weeks been the cause of her reckless actions? If I had told her she was my ketiorra and not ignored her, would she have given the group time to devise a better plan? One that did not involve risking her life.

"No offense, Cara, but is your friend always so impulsive?" Des asked. "Her plan might sound good, but it could get her killed. Shouldn't we be doing something to stop her...or help her?"

Gruesome images of what could happen to Sloane if the males discovered her invaded my mind. "Yes, we should," I snarled, pushing to my feet and trailing after her. By the time I lowered myself over the ledge, Sloane had reached the bottom of the incline. This side of the rocky ridge was much easier to ascend. Years of practiced stealth was on my side, and it did not take me long to shorten the distance between us.

Thankfully, Ryan and the other males were still inside the building, so I made it to the solarveyor unnoticed. Sloane was already inside and standing in the middle of the aisle that extended to the rear of the vehicle. She gasped when I entered, extracting her blade as she spun around to face me. "Garyck," she hissed, returning the knife to its sheath. "What are you doing here?"

"Since you did not give any of us a chance to discuss your plan, I am going with you," I said.

"No, you're not," she said, pushing against my chest. I was a large male, and she did not possess the strength to make me move.

"Yes, I am." Even if I thought it would help or had changed my mind about telling her she was my ketiorra, now was not the time. Sloane had to be the most stubborn female I had ever encountered. Based on my recent actions, I knew she would not listen or believe anything I had to say.

"If the plan is going to work, you need to leave right now, before someone sees you," she said, glancing through the nearest pane that provided a view of the building.

Narrowing my gaze and swishing my tail back and forth did not intimidate her. Instead, she quirked a brow, then gave me her back and moved to the rear of the transport. If the female thought she could dismiss me so easily, she was wrong. I closed the access panel, then kept watch for any movement outside as I trailed after her.

CHAPTER EIGHT

SLOANE

When I'd decided to stow away on the mercs's solarveyor, I hadn't expected anyone to follow me, least of all Garyck. My increased pulse should've slowed down after he'd startled me, but my heart kept a rapid beat. The flutter in my stomach, caused by his nearness, wasn't letting up either.

He was wasting his time if he was here because of the ketaurran honor-bound thing where the males were supposed to protect all females. I'd demonstrated my skills on numerous occasions, so he already knew I could take care of myself. I wasn't about to let myself believe he was here for another reason, one that had something to do with caring.

Unfortunately, arguing with Garyck was moot. The male was more headstrong than me. When he'd reverted to nonverbal communication and started swishing his tail, I knew nothing I did would convince him to leave.

As I moved to the rear of the transport, I didn't see any signs of the weapons containers, which meant they had to be inside the building. They'd need to be transferred into the vehicle before Ryan and his friend could leave. I only hoped I was right about them taking this vehicle and not Des's.

We were running out of time, and if this was going to work, I needed to find a place big enough for us to hide. I opened the panel to one of the lower storage areas, then pulled out the handful of supplies stashed inside. Leaving anything sitting in the aisle would draw attention, so I placed everything in an upper compartment, then got down on my knees and leaned into the space I'd cleared.

"What are you doing?" Garyck asked.

"We can't let the males see us, so I'm clearing out a place to hide."

"In there?" Garyck crouched behind me, infringing on my personal space. Heat surged through my body, the same reaction I had every time he got close to me.

"Yes, why?" I said as I reached inside, searching with my fingertips for the latches I knew would be there. "Do you have a problem with tight spaces?"

"I do not," he huffed as if I'd insulted him.

I removed a panel exposing a hidden compartment. "Good, because it's going to be a tight fit. You can always leave if being crammed inside with me bothers you." His avoidance still hurt, and I wasn't one to hold back on sharing my thoughts. I glanced back at him, trying to gauge his reaction.

His gaze locked with mine, and he swallowed as if searching for an appropriate answer. "Little one...Sloane." He caressed my cheek with the back of his hand. "Being near you has never been a problem."

My cheeks warmed at his affectionate and unexpected response. Before I could ask him to clarify, Garyck pulled back his hand and tipped his chin toward the space I'd created. "How did you know this was here?"

I had a feeling we were in for a long trip, provided we weren't discovered along the way. I was good at biding my time, and if he thought he could evade any future questions by changing the subject, he was mistaken. "During the war, my father and I spent time with some mercs. We smuggled supplies...and other things." I didn't like receiving judgmental comments or disdainful glares, so I didn't talk about my past or the things I'd had to do to survive. I was prepared for both and was surprised when I received neither.

Instead, he placed his hand over mine. "We have all done unpleasant things we are not proud of," he said, his voice laced with regret.

Had something happened to him during the war, something that still burdened him? I didn't appreciate it when others pried into my life, so I wasn't about to pressure him for an answer about his.

"Were Laria and Celeste with you as well?" he asked.

"No, we got separated after the crash and didn't reunite until later. It was right before Burke found us. He took us in and taught us how to fight. You could say we owe him our lives."

"So you planned to repay him by going alone on a deadly mission." His concerned and gentle tone was a little unnerving. It wasn't that I didn't appreciate seeing his softer side; I was used to his gruff demeanor.

"Getting hurt or dying wasn't on my agenda. This was supposed to be a recon adventure to find the weapons, and if I'm lucky,"—I patted my hip—"I'll get to use the new blade I got from Des."

Garyck grunted, amusement flashing in his amber eyes.

I heard voices coming from outside and knew our time had run out. "We need to go." I moved to the side so Garyck could get in first, then crawled in after him. He could've positioned himself so we'd be sitting side by side. Instead, he'd braced his back against the wall, knees bent and facing me. The only open spot available was between his legs, which meant I'd be pressed against his broad chest for the entire trip. A trip that might take hours, maybe last as long as a day.

He quirked a brow, daring me to say anything. I held back a groan as I secured the panel from the inside, then settled in front of him. It irritated me that I fit perfectly. It annoyed me even more that my body welcomed his touch.

He kept his hands on his thighs but wrapped his tail around my middle.

"Really?" I whispered sarcastically.

"It is comfortable," he said, not bothering to remove it.

According to my friends, a ketaurran's tail was extremely sensitive, especially to a female's touch. Using the end of their tail to caress or wrap around a body part was one of the ways a male showed their mate affection. I had no idea why Garyck had possessively encircled my waist. Was it meant to be playful, or was it his way of apologizing for his recent behavior.

Either way, I refused to allow my feelings to interfere with our goal. I'd heard the access panel slide open, and I couldn't tell him to keep his hands and tail to himself without exposing our location. So I did the next best thing possible and skimmed a finger along his scales.

CHAPTER NINE

BURKE

Being in charge wasn't a pleasant job. It meant making decisions that risked the lives of others. Carrying the burden of knowing that an order I'd given had ended someone's life was a responsibility that was hard to bear. When our group had first learned that another war was possible, I swore I wouldn't ask anyone to do anything I wasn't willing to do myself.

I'd thought Sloane's proposal to have someone stowaway on the mercs's solarveyor, hoping it would lead us to the rest of the missing weapons, was a stellar idea. I was about to volunteer to go myself if she hadn't beaten me to it. She didn't share many details about her past or the things she'd done to survive before finally reconnecting with Laria and Celeste again, but I got the impression some of them were distasteful.

I trusted Sloane and knew she was more than capable of handling the task, so I didn't bother to stop her. Garyck's reaction hadn't been a surprise, nor was seeing him trail after her.

I'd been around the ketaurrans enough to spot the

signs after they recognized their mates. I would've bet my best blade that Sloane was Garyck's ketiorra. Why the male refused to tell her, or any of us, was a mystery.

I often wondered if something had happened during the war to cause his less than social behavior and also played a role in why the two of them still weren't together. Because, out of all the couples who'd recently bonded, it was evident that Garyck and Sloane were perfect for each other.

"It looks like Sloane was right," Zaedon said. He'd taken the binoculars and was watching the outpost below. We were all anxious and ready to rush down the rocky slope if Sloane and Garyck were discovered and needed our help. "Ryan and his friend have emerged from the building, carrying containers, and are headed for the other transport."

I crouched closer to the edge, using one of the boulders as cover. Even without the clarity provided by the binoculars, I could still make out what was happening below. It didn't take long for the males to finish loading the containers and drive away from the outpost.

"Guess it's a good thing my solarveyor has a few issues," Des said, smirking.

"Few is an understatement," Cara harrumphed. "But yes, under the circumstances, I'd have to agree."

"Any sign of Everett and the other mercs?" I asked Zaedon. I was pretty sure I knew what had happened to them. And it wasn't pleasant.

"I do not see any movement as yet." Zaedon returned the binoculars to me.

Des glanced in my direction. "You think Ryan and his buddy did something to the other males, don't you?"

"Let's get down there and find out," I said, already heading for the ledge. "I wouldn't be surprised if they suffered the same fate as Doyle."

Once I reached the rear of the first building, I retrieved my blade. I didn't think my friends and I would encounter anyone who might cause us harm, but I liked to be prepared for anything. I led the way, moving along the platform until I reached the closed door at the front of the structure. I paused to listen for signs of movement inside, then shook my head to let the rest of the group know I hadn't heard anything.

As I pushed open the door, I was hit with the scent of freshly drawn blood. Zaedon's sense of smell was more enhanced than mine. He held his breath as he stepped inside.

I moved into the gathering room and found three bodies, one of them Everett's. He was face down on the floor, blood pooling around his neck and head. It appeared as if he'd been attacked from behind and had his throat cut.

One of the other males had taken a hit to his midsection and toppled backward onto a lounger, his hand still clutching the hilt of his unsheathed blade.

The last male lay sprawled at the bottom of a staircase. He must have been descending from the upper level when he received a blast to the chest.

"It looks like they didn't get a chance to defend themselves," Des said, moving to stand next to me.

No one commented. We all knew this was the kind of carnage many people would face if we didn't find and destroy the laser weapons. "We need to get going," I said, thinking about Garyck and Sloane as I started to leave the building.

"What about them?" Cara asked, hitching a thumb at the males.

"There is nothing we can do for them now," I said. "We don't have time to bury them."

The males knew the risks when they helped Doyle take the laser blasters. Their traitorous plan involved ending many lives. As far as I was concerned, they'd gotten what they deserved. My main objective now was tracking down Garyck and Sloane, then doing my best to keep them safe.

"Zaedon, check the back rooms and make sure the viewing panels are secured so no wildlife can get inside," I said. Once outside, I turned to Des. "I need you to go back to the settlement and fill Khyron in on everything that's happened. Tell him he'll need to send some people out here to take care of the bodies."

"You want me to give the drezdarr an update?" Des asked. "Are you sure someone else can't do it?"

"Are you afraid of Khyron?" Cara asked.

"No, I'm worried how Laria and Celeste will react when they find out about Sloane."

"I do not blame you," Zaedon chuckled. "The females can be very scary."

"Please tell me the rest of you are going after Sloane and Garyck," Des said.

"Absolutely," Cara said.

"They already have a head start, so how do you plan to track them?" Des said as he stepped off the platform.

"The bag Sloane pulled out of her travel pack contained zapharite stones," Cara said.

Des snapped his fingers. "The crumbs she mentioned."

"Yep." Cara nodded.

"Clever."

I glanced at the darkening sky in the distance. "We should be able to follow them without too much trouble unless that storm decides to head in our direction."

"Tracking them is the easy part," Zaedon said. "It is not knowing what awaits us when we reach our destination that concerns me."

"You and me both," I said as I headed for the transport. I wasn't interested in doing any more rock climbing. "Des, you can drop us off by the other vehicle on your way back to the settlement."

CHAPTER TEN

GARYCK

The space inside Sloane's hiding spot was tight. My decision to sit, so her body was pressed against mine, might not have been wise, but I did not mind…much.

Having her between my thighs caused my shaft to harden. If she noticed, she did not say anything. Being reassured that she was my ketiorra with each inhale of her intoxicating scent was worth any discomfort I endured.

I should not have been surprised that she knew about my tail's sensitivity or that she would use it against me when I tried to snuggle her closer. It seemed that ignoring Sloane had caused her more pain than I had intended and would not be easily forgiven.

Having her close and realizing that her life was at risk should we fail made me question my recent decision to avoid her. If I could redo the last few weeks, I would tell her how much she meant to me. How much I wanted to keep her in my life. How I craved to claim her as my mate, to make our bond permanent.

Now I might never get the chance, and my regret about my choices continued to gnaw at me. I promised myself I would do everything to correct my mistakes once we returned to the settlement, provided we survived our current mission.

Being hidden behind a metal wall did not eliminate the muffled footsteps of the males after they entered the transport. The loud thud that sounded close to the outside panel had my chest tightening and Sloane's body tensing.

"We need to hurry with the rest of the weapons," Ryan said. "I don't want to be around when Burke and the others get here." He confirmed that the noise I heard was made by a container filled with laser blasters being placed on the floor. It was also a relief to hear that he was unaware that my friends and I had already arrived.

I remembered Ryan's interest in Sloane, and the possessive part of my nature wanted him to see her settled next to my body, to know that she was my mate. Lately, my tail had a mind of its own and started snaking its way toward her midsection again. The sharp press of Sloane's elbow against my ribs was enough incentive for me to control the urge and focus on the activities outside the storage compartment.

Hopefully, once Ryan and the other males finished loading the containers, they would leave them where they were and not decide to store them inside the lower storage area.

The panel Sloane had slid back into place would hide our location, but the threat of discovery heightened my stress. Even if our presence wasn't discovered, having the containers stacked in the storage unit would make getting out of the vehicle difficult, maybe even impossible.

As soon as their footsteps faded, Sloane exhaled, her shoulders sagging. "That was close," she whispered.

"I agree," I muttered, knowing that wrapping her in my arms and telling her I would keep her safe would be unwelcome.

Silence filled the air, and minutes passed before I heard movement again and the thump of another container hitting the floor. The males made one more trip before the engine rumbled to life and the metal beneath my backside vibrated. Since I had not heard any other voices besides Ryan's and his friend, I assumed Everett and the other mercs would not be joining them and were most likely dead.

Other than the small amount of light coming from a gap between the back panel and the floor, the interior was cast in darkness. Once we were moving, it was difficult to determine the direction we traveled unless the vehicle shifted as it made a hard turn.

There was only one road leading into the outpost, so the males would need to leave the same way they arrived. When whoever was piloting the transport slowed and headed left, I knew we were traveling along the outskirts of the Quaddrien, not toward the settlement.

Putting distance between themselves and the outpost seemed to be a priority because the vehicle moved at an accelerated speed, only slowing to accommodate bad conditions on the road.

Sloane rolled on one hip and pulled the small bag she'd grabbed earlier from her pocket. I watched, confused at first, as she retrieved a zapharite stone, lighting up the interior. She tipped her head and winked at me, then wedged it through the small gap between the back panel and the floor. We were not sitting directly over the engine compartment, so the small rock fell to the ground underneath the vehicle.

The earlier comment she'd made about crumbs now made sense. Unless the weather turned drastic, the small rocks glowed and would leave a clear trail for our friends to follow. Sloane constantly amazed me, and I grinned, proud of my mate's ingenuity.

I relaxed against the wall, remembering what Sloane had said about her sire. She had never mentioned him before, and I wondered if he had perished during the war as did many other loved ones.

I longed to hear her voice and ask her questions about her past. The sounds coming from the engine would no doubt drown out any conversation we had, but I was not willing to risk making any noise.

Movement was limited, and it wasn't long before the muscles in my legs had cramped. Without being able to see the sun's position, it was hard to determine how much time had passed since we left the outpost. I knew it was not evening because the light coming through the gap near the floor had dimmed but not faded completely.

Some time had passed since Sloane had dropped a stone through the gap. She had dozed, and I did not wish to wake her. I slowly tugged on the bag she grasped in her hand. As soon as the bag pulled free, she jerked awake and reached for her hip. My thigh was in the way and received the grip she'd meant for her blade's hilt.

I had to shake the bag in front of Sloane's face for several seconds before she snapped out of her sleepy haze and remembered where she was and why. I missed the contact of having her hand pressed against my leg the instant she removed it to snatch the bag.

I pointed at the gap, letting her know it was time to drop another stone. With a nod, she complied, then settled comfortably against my body. Her soft moan, which I was certain Sloane was unaware she had made, filled me with satisfaction.

***

SLOANE

By the time Ryan's transport jerked to a stop, I'd taken a nap, dropped three more stones, and couldn't feel my backside. I could, however, still feel Garyck's warmth along the areas where his body touched mine.

It was a good thing I sat facing away from him. Memories of the erection he'd sported for quite some time after I'd first settled in front of him brought a smug grin to my face.

The fact that he'd reacted to me so easily confirmed I hadn't imagined the attraction between us. It only made the issue of him avoiding me even more confusing than it had been.

After waiting until I was sure Ryan and his friend had exited the vehicle, I shifted and sat on my knees.

"Do you have a plan for getting out of this vehicle without being seen?" Garyck asked. There was no judgment or sarcasm in his question. He sounded as if he was willing to follow me without stipulating any conditions.

"Uh-huh," I said, pulling a stone out of my bag, then holding the rock out to him. "Would you mind holding this so I can see what I'm doing?"

I retrieved my blade, then leaned over his bent leg and used the tip to pry the back panel of the compartment free. Because I'd been nestled tightly against Garyck, any movements I made involved rubbing against him. The light from the stone cast shadows in the corners, but I had a clear view of his face. Judging by his smirk, he seemed to be enjoying the additional contact immensely.

"Little one, I do not believe I will fit through that opening."

After glancing at the narrow space, I realized he was right and groaned. I had a petite build and had squeezed through similar holes on other vehicles, so I wasn't worried about fitting.

Besides being distracted by his arrival, having Garyck accompany me hadn't been part of my plan, so I hadn't taken his size into account. We both knew the only way he was getting off the solarveyor was by using the main access panel.

Though I'd never admit it, a part of me was glad he'd tagged along. I didn't care what had caused the distance between us. He was with me now, and we had a job to do.

I wasn't going to risk something happening to him because we separated. "I'm not leaving without you."

"Yes, you are." Before I had time to react, Garyck scooped me into his arms, then helped me through the opening, feet first. As soon as my boots touched the ground, I spun around and grabbed the frame, ready to crawl back inside.

"Garyck, this is my plan," I said through gritted teeth. "You can't order me around and expect me to comply. Whatever we face, we're doing it together."

"And we will, but now you must go and find the weapons."

"Not happening." I tried to pull myself up, but he gripped my nape. His lips captured mine with a possessive kiss that stole my breath and wrecked my concentration. It also ended too quickly.

"I will be right behind you." His words lacked conviction. We both knew the odds of him getting off the transport without being seen dropped by the second.

He freed my hands from the frame. Before I could argue, he set the panel back in place, keeping me from getting back inside. I couldn't believe he'd distracted me with a kiss. Even if the kiss was better than anything I'd ever imagined, I wanted to throttle the male and had to stop myself from pounding on the metal.

Finding the weapons was important, but so was Garyck, and I wasn't leaving him. I crouched close to the ground so I wouldn't be seen, then slowly eased forward to take in my surroundings. The sun was setting, the visible portion of the sky, not filled with dark clouds, was a darker green than normal.

Other than taking the road that I knew took us past the Quaddrien, the vehicle hadn't made any drastic turns prior to our arrival. It was easy to determine the direction we'd been traveling.

Any hopes I had about help coming soon diminished when I glimpsed the heavy storm clouds hovering over the same area in the distance. If the rain was coming down hard as I suspected, the stone trail I'd left would be swallowed up by the thick mud that formed when water mixed with the sandy dirt.

Just once, it would be nice if something went my way and I didn't always have to do things the hard way.

I've never been to this area. From what I could see of the buildings, the place didn't look like any town I'd ever visited, more of a secluded outpost, only with more structures.

Checking the other direction, I saw several more vehicles parked nearby. I hoped that someone maintained them and kept their solars charged because Garyck and I would eventually need a way out of here. We couldn't use the vehicle I was hiding under since the solars would be partially drained from our recent trip.

I heard male voices heading in my direction, one of them Ryan's. They must've been returning for the weapons containers, which meant I'd be stuck under the solarveyor for a while longer.

I eased back into the shadows, worried that Garyck might get caught if he'd already crawled out of the storage compartment. Ryan's friend was either in charge or ranked high on the list of whoever was in command.

They'd gathered quite a few weapons. If they planned to start a war, they'd need a lot of people to wield them. Without looking inside all the buildings, I had no way of knowing how many had been recruited. Distraction ideas rushed through my mind, but I couldn't come up with anything that didn't include me exposing my location.

I already knew at least one of the males working with Ryan was a ketaurran and assumed there were more. They had better hearing than humans, so when the males stopped not far from where I was hiding, I slowed my breathing to prevent detection. All I could see was the bottom portion of their pant-covered legs and boots.

"Take the containers and put them with the others." I

recognized the voice as belonging to Cara's mysterious male. He remained standing where he was while the others headed to the front of the vehicle.

Scraping and scuffling echoed from the metal floor above my head. Minutes later, the males exited the vehicle and passed near my spot, heading for a building on the right. If I'd overheard correctly, the laser blasters were now all in the same place. The valuable information wouldn't be helpful unless I could find a way to reach the building and dismantle the weapons.

A few minutes later, someone approached from the opposite direction. The male limped and dragged his tail across the dirt as if the appendage had been injured.

"Draejek, I take it things went well, and you have recovered the remaining weapons," the injured male said, his voice deep and gravelly. I finally had a name for the mysterious ketaurran my friends and I had been searching for.

"Yes, Sarus," Draejek said.

I clamped a hand over my mouth to stifle a gasp. I'd never met or seen Sarus, even from a distance. There'd been rumors he'd died in the war, that his supporters were the ones who wanted to continue his fight. The vryndarr, especially Jardun, never believed the stories of his death and would be happy to know they were right. At least about their suppositions, not that the older male had survived.

A lot of lives had been lost because of Sarus, my father included. If I thought I had a chance of making it to him without being stopped, I'd crawl out from under the transport and run my new blade through his despicable heart.

"And the males who believed it wise to double-cross me?" Sarus asked.

"They have been disposed of," Draejek said.

"Good, good," Sarus said. "Come, we will have a meal with ale and discuss my plans to overthrow my sibling's offspring so I can take over as the new drezdarr."

The males could do all the strategizing they wanted. It wasn't going to do them any good because I planned to do a massive amount of thwarting as soon as I could get out from under the transport.

.

CHAPTER ELEVEN

GARYCK

Releasing Sloane from our kiss, then forcing her to stay underneath the transport had to be one of the most difficult things I had ever done. It was the first time my lips touched hers, and I relished the remaining tingle the contact with her soft skin had caused. None of my imaginings came close to our actual yet brief encounter, and I was left wanting more.

Now was not the time to entertain those kinds of thoughts. I needed to remain focused, to ensure that at least one of us found the weapons and made sure that no one ever got a chance to use them.

I heard voices outside, but they were muffled. I could not tell that it was Ryan and another male who had returned until they entered the transport and discussed moving the containers.

Once I was sure all the containers had been carried away, I removed the panel that Sloane had set in place to hide our location within the storage area. My arms scraped along the frame, so extracting my body from the unit was harder than when I had entered.

I pulled myself into a standing position, making sure I was not seen through any of the viewing panes. My body ached, so I took a few seconds to stretch my muscles and wait for the tingling sensation in my legs to pass.

Unsure what I would encounter once I left the transport, I remained alert as I crouched and crept toward the front of the vehicle.

I could not tell if Sloane had remained underneath or if she had followed my instructions and gone in search of the weapons. I had learned the hard way that she could be extremely defiant and was not good at following orders, even more so if they came from me.

I was glad the males had not bothered to close the access panel when they left, making my departure less cumbersome. I was about to slip outside when I heard a familiar voice and froze.

My heart raced. My chest constricted, the pressure making it difficult to breathe. Horrible memories from the past exploded in my mind. The faces of friends I had lost and the hours of torturous pain I had endured felt like it had happened yesterday. I had spent an immeasurable amount of time hoping the male had died, yet instinctively knowing he had not.

I took a quiet step back, then peered through the viewing pane, trying to get a glimpse of the male who had ruined so many lives. Ryan and the weapons containers were nowhere in sight, but Sarus stood conversing with Cara's mysterious male.

He may have survived numerous battles, but he had not gone unscathed. One side of his face was covered with a scar that ran from his cheekbone to his jaw. He favored one leg, and his tail, no longer capable of moving on its own, dragged along the ground like a lifeless appendage.

The male had frequently vocalized his hatred of humans, so I was shocked to discover that he had some working for him. I did not believe losing the war had changed his views.

Control and manipulation were his honed skills of choice. Making promises that he never planned to keep was a method he used to get what he wanted. It was probably the tactic he used with Ryan to get him to infiltrate the settlement and betray his people. I would wager all the blades I possessed that his plan to remove Khyron as drezdarr involved disposing of all the humans who had helped him afterward.

Now that I knew Sarus was alive, it was difficult to control the rage rippling through my body. Sloane was clever and elusive, but all I could think about was him somehow getting his hands on her. If he did, would his orders include torturing her, maybe doing something worse, like passing her around to all his males before ending her life?

The thought of anyone touching or harming my ketiorra was overwhelming, and I reacted without thinking. "Sarus!" I yelled, retrieving my blade as I jumped to the ground.

I was so focused on finishing the male and preventing another war that I had not considered the possibility of anyone being armed with a laser blaster. The mysterious male stepped into view and pulled one of the weapons from inside his jacket. He leveled it at my chest before Sarus had finished removing the long blade from his belt.

"Draejek," Sarus snarled as he held up a hand. "Do not fire. I want him alive."

The male did not appear pleased by the order but acknowledged his compliance with a tip of his head.

Ryan, along with two other males I assumed had helped him move the weapons containers, appeared on my right, all brandishing blades. It seemed that Sarus did not trust anyone other than Draejek to carry a blaster. It had been a wise choice, one that worked in their favor until Cara had seen Draejek's weapon.

This place had to be fairly isolated and not visited by vendors who sold their goods at the traders markets. In order to feed the males living here, someone would need to venture to the closest community to stock their supplies. Being armed with blasters would draw unwanted attention, and eventually, the news would reach the drezdarr.

Anger followed by concern flashed across Ryan's features. My appearance had to be a problem because he nervously glanced at Sarus, no doubt concerned about the ramifications.

"Garyck," Sarus said. "I assume you have come for the human weapons and already know they cause considerable damage. Unless you would like a demonstration, I suggest you drop your blade."

I gripped the hilt of my knife tighter and considered my options. I would not hold the title of vryndarr if I did not have excellent fighting skills or was adept at throwing my blade and hitting my target. Sarus was also a skilled warrior, prepared for any type of attack, and could easily dodge my attempt.

I remembered Cara saying that a single laser blast could kill. I was not familiar with the weapon's range and did not know if I would be able to avoid being hit. As tempted as I was to wipe the taunting sneer from Draejek's face, I refused to let him influence my decision.

Had I been alone, I would have taken my chances. If something happened to me, then Sloane would be on her own. Her life was too valuable for me to risk. As soon as I dropped my blade, one of the males pulled out a stun stick and jabbed me in the ribs.

Typically, the jolt would have been annoying, but this was excruciating and brought me to my knees. By the time I realized the stick had been modified, my vision blurred, and darkness claimed me.

CHAPTER TWELVE

SLOANE

Draeck. The ketaurran curse word raced through my mind after I saw Garyck drop to the ground outside the solarveyor. My chest tightened, the pain almost unbearable. If Sarus hadn't ordered Draejek not to use his blaster, Garyck would be dead.

Normally, stun sticks couldn't produce a jolt strong enough to take down a vryndarr. This one had to be one of the modified versions my friends and I had encountered before. I knew it had only knocked Garyck out, but rational thought was difficult. I resisted the urge to rush to his side and make sure he was all right.

I couldn't believe he'd exposed himself by going after Sarus. I wanted to know what he'd been thinking, why he didn't wait until everyone had left. He possessed the stealth of a predator and could've easily avoided detection.

"Check inside the transport," Sarus ordered. "See if there were any others with him."

Even if they found the place where Garyck and I were hiding, they wouldn't know I'd been with him or that I'd dropped underneath the vehicle.

I heard footsteps and rummaging around above my head. A few minutes later, a male called out to Sarus, "There's no one else in here."

"What should we do with him?" Draejek asked.

"Put him in the holding cell for now," Sarus said. "We will question him when he awakens."

I lowered my body closer to the ground to get a better view of where they were taking Garyck. I watched two males grab him under the arms and drag him across the compound to a smaller structure that sat away from the rest of the buildings.

After the males exited a few minutes later without Garyck, one of them braced a thick wooden bar across the door to secure it from the outside. I wanted to help him but didn't want to risk exposing myself or being captured.

Garyck would be unconscious for quite some time, so trying to rescue him now wouldn't do me any good. I hated leaving him behind, but I might not get another opportunity to find the weapons and hopefully figure out a way to destroy them. Sarus must have known Garyck would be down for a while as well, which explained why he locked him up instead of questioning him.

Once I completed my task, I'd come back for Garyck. As soon as I got us both to safety, we were definitely discussing his reckless behavior. Now that he'd announced his arrival, I'd have to be extra careful.

The remnants of sunlight were quickly fading. The structures were roughly constructed, and I didn't see any signs of exterior lighting. Moving around without difficulty posed a problem, but the approaching nightfall improved my chances of not being seen.

I found it odd that Sarus didn't leave any guards posted outside Garyck's building or anywhere else that I could see. Maybe this place was so secluded that he wasn't worried anyone would be able to find it.

After crawling out from underneath the transport, I checked to make sure no one was lurking in the shadows, then hurried to the nearest building. The exterior had two visible panes, both shuttered and spaced an equal distance apart on the same wall. Light shone through the cracks on the nearest one, and I could hear voices coming from inside.

I crouched low and eased my way to the rear of the building. Once there, I crept to the structure where I'd seen the males take the containers filled with weapons. I'd hoped there'd be an accessible pane I could use to sneak inside and rolled my eyes when all I found was a solid wall of wood.

After moving to the far end of the building, I peered around the corner. There was a four-foot walkway between this structure and the next. The gap between them was cast in shadows, so I pulled a zapharite stone from the bag in my pocket to help me see better. The light provided was dim, but I could make out the frame surrounding a pane midway along the wall.

After retrieving the dagger from inside my boot, I went to work on freeing the right side of the shutter. I hadn't heard any movement since Sarus and the other males went inside, but it didn't stop me from pausing and listening every time the wood creaked. After what seemed like forever, I was able to move the panel aside.

Being short had its benefits, but squeezing through the opening without kicking off the ground first, wasn't one of them. Landing on the floor once I managed to get inside wasn't exactly graceful, but I didn't think I'd end up with any bruises. After dusting off my pants, I flattened out my hand and used the stone to see around the room.

There were eight containers stacked two high sitting on the floor along one wall. On the other side of the room was a table displaying numerous blades in various lengths and widths. Ketaurran craftsmanship was impressive. It was hard to resist the urge to run my fingertip across some of the smooth metal surfaces.

Besides the blades, there were also three stun sticks

similar to the one used on Garyck. I grabbed one, thinking it might come in handy, and at the same time, hoping no one would notice that it was gone.

After hooking the stick to my belt, I returned my attention to the containers, wondering how many of the weapons had been removed. It wouldn't do our cause any good if Sarus had already handed out a bunch of the blasters. Even a handful in the wrong hands would do a lot of damage.

So far, Draejek was the only person I'd seen with a blaster. I couldn't get a good enough view to tell if the other males had been armed and needed to know for sure. Before doing anything else, I needed visual verification of how many weapons were missing from the containers.

I started by pulling the top box on the left off the stack, then lifted the lid. From the containers my friends and I had confiscated some time ago, I already knew how many weapons should be stacked inside and was glad to see that they were all there.

I systematically worked through the rest of the containers by placing the top ones on the floor and removing all the lids. I was relieved to discover that only one container appeared to be missing a weapon, which had to be the one in Draejek's possession.

I thought about creeping back to the building where Sarus and the other males had gathered to see if I could overhear the plans for his attack. If things went awry and I got caught, Garyck and I might end up dead, so I passed on implementing the idea.

Since sneaking the containers onto a transport was out of the question, disabling the weapons was my best option. Thankfully, I'd been able to rely on Cara's mechanical expertise. She'd shown my friends and me how to easily recalibrate a mechanism inside a laser blaster that would cause it to explode. Modifying one weapon should be enough to destroy all of them.

Before I blew up this building, I'd have to rescue

Garyck. I'd barely made it to the pane so I could crawl back outside when the only door leading into the building creaked open, and someone stepped inside. I spun around, the soft glow of my stone enough for me to make out the male's features. "Ryan?" I asked, glancing behind him to make sure he was alone.

"Hello, Sloane," he said, smirking. "I had a feeling Garyck hadn't made the trip alone." He took a few steps closer. "I'm sorry it had to be you."

He almost sounded sincere, but I didn't believe it for a minute. "Why's that?"

"Sarus hates his nephew...and anyone associated with him," Ryan said. "Your chances of survival aren't looking very good." He ran his tongue along his lower lip. "Unless you'd like me to persuade Sarus to put you under my care."

Ryan's idea of care translated into sharing his bed. Bile churned in my stomach, and it took everything I had not to cringe. "Thanks, but I think I'll take my chances."

Ryan gazed at the open containers scattered across the floor. "You've been busy."

There was no point in denying what I'd been doing, so I shrugged.

Unfortunately, a couple of the containers were located between him and me. He walked over to the nearest one, picked up a weapon, and aimed it at my chest.

"You wouldn't shoot me, would you?" I asked though I didn't doubt for a second that he would.

"I won't if you cooperate." He pointed at my waist with his weapon. "You can start by handing over the stun stick."

Ryan was observant, and I'd hoped with the limited lighting that he hadn't noticed my recent acquisition. I groaned and reluctantly handed the stick over to him.

He tucked it in the back of his pants, seemingly amused. "The blade next."

"But it's new, and I didn't get a chance to use it yet," I

said, pouting.

"I'm sorry about that."

"Funny, you don't sound very sorry."

"Yeah, well, because I'm not," he said. "Now, take it out slowly and place it on the floor. And use your left hand," he added when I started to grab the hilt with my right.

I gave Ryan points for intelligence. He'd no longer be standing if he'd let me remove the knife with my predominant hand. It was too bad he didn't know me as well as he thought. There was no way I'd let him deliver me to Sarus willingly, and I wasn't going to abandon Garyck, even if his current situation was his fault.

"I'm curious," I said, dropping my stone on the floor, then squatting to place my knife next to it. "What did Sarus promise you that was worth betraying all of us?" I couldn't think of anything that would justify what he was doing, so the answer didn't matter. I only asked because I needed a distraction.

When he swiped his hand along the side of his head, I pulled the dagger from my boot. I released the blade with an upward motion, then rolled to the side to avoid being shot. I could survive an injury to one of my limbs, but a blast to the chest would kill me.

Luckily, Ryan didn't have his finger on the firing button when I'd thrown my blade. His body jerked from the impact, but he didn't accidentally release a blast. He made a choking sound and stared at me in disbelief. After dropping the weapon, Ryan gripped the hilt of my dagger. Pulling out the blade seemed to hurry things along because it was the last thing he did before falling to the floor.

I didn't enjoy taking a life and avoided doing it whenever possible. There was too much at stake, and Ryan had known the risks when he'd decided to join up with Sarus, so the regret I felt didn't last long.

"Ryan, are you out here?" a male's voice echoed from outside.

Whoever was looking for him must not have seen the open door yet, and I wanted to keep it that way. In order to close the door, I needed to move Ryan's body. Using all the strength I could muster, I grabbed his ankles and dragged him a few more feet into the room. Not an easy task, considering he weighed a lot more than I did and wasn't cooperating.

Once I got him out of the way, I quietly closed the door, then blocked it with a container. I needed to get to Garyck before Ryan's body was discovered. My original plan to return and modify a blaster wasn't going to work.

After prying my dagger out of Ryan's hand, I swiped both sides of the blade on his pants. It seemed a little heartless, but I wasn't about to put the dagger back in my boot with blood on it. Next, I grabbed a weapon out of the nearest container, then used the blade's tip to make the necessary adjustments.

If I'd followed Cara's instructions correctly, I figured I had about ten minutes before the laser overheated. I didn't want to be anywhere in the vicinity when the weapon started a chain reaction that would cause an explosion.

After placing the weapon in a centrally located container, I slipped the stone back in my pocket, then grabbed the framework around the open pane and hauled myself through the opening.

Dropping to the ground outside didn't go any smoother than when I'd crawled inside. I stayed close to the wall, listening for any sign of movement, and didn't hear any. The male who'd been looking for Ryan must have gone in the other direction.

After giving the area one last glance, I spotted the prison building and started running. As I raced through the darkness, I hoped Garyck was awake and alert enough to make it to one of the transports.

CHAPTER THIRTEEN

GARYCK

As I sifted through the haze in my mind, I could not decide what hurt more; the throbbing in my head or the sharp pain where I'd been jabbed in the side with the stun stick. Something shackled around my wrist hindered my attempt to raise my arm and rub my temples.

I forced my eyelids open and found myself lying on a cold, hard floor and chained to a nearby wall, the length too short to allow standing. Ignoring the stiffened muscles in my back, I rolled into a sitting position, then took in my surroundings.

Zapharite stones had been mounted on two of the walls. They provided enough light for me to see that the room was small, had no panes, and resembled the interior of the holding cell back at the settlement.

A single door was the only way in or out and was most likely braced from the outside. The interior had not been designed for comfort. The only piece of furniture was a wooden chair sitting on the opposite side of the room and out of reach.

The relief I felt at not finding Sloane with me quickly

faded. Just because she was not being held in this room did not mean she had not been captured.

Escape would have been easy if my blades had not been confiscated, including the dagger I kept in my boot. Frustrated by my current situation and the overwhelming need to find her, I fisted my hands around the chains and pulled as hard as I could. The wall mount groaned but after several attempts, refused to budge.

I heard scraping on the outside of the door and tensed. I assumed it was Sarus and some of his males returning to question me, which would escalate to torture since I would not supply them with any answers. The chains were short and prevented me from standing to my full height, but I refused to let that keep me from defending myself.

Night had arrived during my unconscious state. A darkened silhouette was all I could see of the person, much shorter than I had expected, standing in the doorway. A few seconds later, Sloane stepped inside. "Garyck." Her sweet voice echoed through the room.

"Little one," I said. "You are unharmed?"

She propped a long, rectangular board against the inside wall and closed the door. "Of course, I'm not hurt." I had never been happier to hear the sarcasm in her voice or have her roll those beautiful blue eyes at me. "But obviously, you're not." She glanced around the room, then continued inside. "What the draeck were you thinking, going after Sarus like that?" She punched my shoulder.

I had already chastised myself for lacking better judgment and would gladly endure any additional scolding she was prepared to give me.

"You could've been killed."

Her anger was laced with caring as if my foolish actions had caused her a great deal of pain. "I—"

"Save it," she said, cutting me off. "We don't have time to discuss it right now." Sloane retrieved the dagger from her boot. "We can talk about it later." She went to work on the cuff clamped to my wrist. "If we make it out of here, that is," she muttered as an afterthought, and more to herself than me.

Escaping on all of our missions was always a concern. Something in her tone suggested she was more troubled about the situation than usual.

Sloane paused after removing the first cuff, then frowned as she gently brushed her fingertips over the raw and reddened marks my attempts to free myself had left on my skin.

The injury was minor when compared to others I had sustained. "It is nothing," I said, placing my hand over hers.

"Glad to hear it." Sloane pulled her hand free and went to work on the other cuff.

She bit her lower lip, concentrating on her task. "We will also be talking about that other thing you did before you shoved me under the transport."

I grinned. Sloane was not one to hold back how she felt about anything. I found it curious that she did not specifically mention the kiss.

"Thank you," I said as soon as she unclasped the cuff and discarded it on the floor. I pulled her into my arms, inhaling her aroma. She was alive, and that was all that mattered.

"You're welcome, but we need to go." She squirmed until I released her, then headed for the door. After briefly stopping to peer outside, she grabbed the board again, then exited into the night.

We did not want Sarus, or any of his males, to discover my escape any sooner than necessary. While Sloane closed the door and replaced the board to make it look as if I was still housed inside, I scanned the area, noting the cluster of buildings located apart from this one.

"The weapons?" I asked. Sloane was thorough and would have already explored the compound before coming for me.

"In that building over there." She pointed toward the

structure situated on the far left of the others.

Before I could take a step, Sloane grabbed my hand. "No, you can't go that way."

"Why not?" I asked though I let her pull me in a different direction. "Little one, what is going on?"

"Later. Right now, we need to get to a transport and get out of here as quickly as possible."

We had almost reached the structures on the opposite side of the compound when a door opened on the building near the transports. I tugged Sloane into the shadows of the walkway between the closest buildings, then pressed her back against the wall, using my body to shield her.

"Any sign of Ryan?" Sarus asked, stepping outside to speak with a human male.

"No," the male answered. "Maybe he's with the prisoner. I haven't checked there or the weapons building yet."

"Ryan would have no reason to be in either of those places," Sarus growled his discontent. "Continue searching. Take several others with you."

The male nodded and hurried off at the same time Draejek joined Sarus.

"Do you think there is a problem?" Draejek asked.

"I do not know," Sarus said. "But now might be a good time to gain some information from our prisoner."

"Do you think the vryndarr will answer your questions?" Draejek asked.

"Probably not." Sarus patted his blade. "But I will enjoy trying to extract them anyway. Maybe this time I will be able to break him."

My body stiffened, remembering what the male had others do to me the last time I had been his prisoner. Things I wanted to remain in the past. Things I would rather Sloane not know about me. Rather than be disgusted and pull away after what she had overheard, she placed a hand on my arm. Her gentle squeeze had a calming effect.

As I watched Sarus and Draejek head toward the building we had recently exited, the urge to finish what I had started earlier grew stronger but not as strong as the need to keep Sloane safe.

It would not be long before the males Sarus had ordered to continue searching for Ryan to circle back in our direction again. If Ryan was also somewhere nearby, I did not want to run into him either. "We move once they are inside," I whispered, then took Sloane's hand, not willing to risk being separated from her again.

She nodded, and as soon as Draejek removed the locking brace and pushed on the door, we raced for the closest solarveyor. Getting inside was easy. The males had not engaged any security for the access panel, maybe because of the compound's isolated location.

"Find him!" was all I heard of Sarus's angry shout before Sloane sealed us inside.

I slid into the pilot's seat, ran my hand over the controls, and had the engine rumbling to life within seconds.

"Drive," Sloane said, grabbing hold of the hull's framework and nervously glancing out the pane. "And fast."

I engaged the accelerator, and the vehicle jerked into motion. Though I wished the exterior lights mounted to the front of the transport's exterior were brighter, they provided enough light for me to see where we were going.

Unfortunately, it meant that the solars were not fully charged. We would not get far unless we stopped and let the transport absorb the rays produced by sunlight. We were also headed in a different direction than when we had arrived. I was not familiar with this area and had no idea where we would end up.

"Does your plan include returning for the weapons?" I asked Sloane. "Sarus will move them long before Burke and the others arrive." I had scented rainfall in the air and worried that they might not arrive at all.

"Nope, it doesn't," Sloane said, her devious tone making me wary.

"Why?"

"I rigged one of the blasters to—" Before she could finish, a loud boom erupted behind us.

CHAPTER FOURTEEN

GARYCK

When we left the compound, I had taken the only visible road available. The sky seemed darker than usual, more so on the horizon. Some storms appeared without warning, and I feared we would soon encounter heavy rainfall. If that happened, the sandy dirt would turn into slippery mud, making traveling at a rapid speed dangerous.

It was difficult to gauge how much time had passed since Sloane and I had heard the explosion. I would never purposely wish anyone dead, but in this instance, I found myself hoping that there were no survivors. It would mean the end to the future threat of war.

We traveled in silence, tension thrumming through the interior of the solarveyor. Sloane had remained standing near the access panel so she could keep watch through the viewing pane at the rear of the vehicle.

"Anything?" I asked. I wanted to return to Sarus's compound and confirm that all the laser blasters had been destroyed. Draejek might have been the only male I had seen with a weapon, but that did not mean others had not been given out. Others that could not continue to exist.

Until things between Sloane and me were resolved and I could think clearly, I did not want to drag her into another life-threatening situation. I already knew the obstinate female would refuse to stay behind, so there was no point in discussing it with her.

"Nothing yet," she said.

It was not like her to remain deep in thought for such a long time. Because of the distance I had created between us, I immediately assumed Sloane was thinking of Ryan. She had befriended the male and spent additional time with him. His interest in her had been obvious, but I did not know if she reciprocated the same feelings. The male's betrayal would bother her, but would she be concerned about his survival?

Instead of requesting the information outright, I asked, "Why were the males searching for Ryan?"

She shifted sideways to continue watching outside and give me her attention simultaneously. "He figured out that you weren't alone and decided to go looking for that person," she said, her voice tinged with regret.

It sounded as if Sarus was unaware of Sloane's presence. If he had known that Ryan was looking for someone else, surely he would have mentioned it when he ordered the male to continue searching for him.

Was it possible Ryan hadn't shared his suspicions, that he had wanted to confirm them first before saying anything? If that was the case, then maybe when Sarus discovered I had escaped, he believed Ryan had been the one to help me.

"And you know this how?"

"He found me with the weapons…before I came to get you," she said. "I'm afraid he tried to separate me from my new blade, so things didn't end well for him."

"I am sorry," I said. I felt bad that Sloane had been forced to take his life. Ryan had betrayed us, so I would not mourn his death.

Sloane shrugged. "It was inevitable. If not by me, then

by one of our teammates." There was nothing more either of us could say on the matter, so she returned to staring into the darkness behind us. Not long after that, soft pings echoed from the hull's exterior, the noise gradually getting louder as the rainfall increased.

"Great," she muttered. "That's all we need."

I grunted my agreement. If the rain continued, traveling would become dangerous.

"Suggestions?" she asked sarcastically.

"I will go as far as the remaining power in the solars and road conditions will allow," I said. "Then we will have to stop and wait until morning before deciding how to proceed."

"That's kind of risky if someone's following us, isn't it?"

"Maybe, but if the roads get bad, they will be forced to stop as well."

Sloane slid into the seat next to me. "We can only hope."

As I feared, the rain continued falling, the heavy wall of water decreasing visibility. The road narrowed, and driving conditions worsened. Lowering the speed did not seem to matter. As I'd predicted, the sandy dirt had transformed into a mud that made maneuvering difficult. The rocks on our left had grown into a towering wall. The ground on our right had darkened, and I caught glimpses of a ravine running along the edge.

Something collided with the rear of the transport, causing it to jerk forward. I tightened my grip on the steering controls to keep the vehicle away from the ravine.

Sloane was thrown sideways but managed to stay in her seat. "What the..." she asked as she righted herself.

"There is someone behind us." I pressed on the accelerator. It was not a wise choice, but the only option available if I wanted to avoid being forced into the ravine.

Sloane pushed out of her seat.

"Where are you going?" I asked. Moving around was

not safe, especially if we were rammed again. It did not help that the interior lighting that drew its power from the solars had dimmed some time ago, and she could not see in the dark as well as I could.

"To get a better look at what's behind us." She used the hull's metal framework on her side of the solarveyor to work her way back to the viewing pane. "It's too dark out there. All I can see are the front lights of another vehicle."

Our transport started sliding, forcing me to lower the speed again. The other vehicle would also be struggling with the deteriorating conditions, which did not necessarily mean the male operating it would adjust his speed. It helped that we had entered an area where the road curved to accommodate the rocky terrain. Once it straightened out, the transport behind us would have an advantage again.

"I remember the last time we were in a pursuit situation like this," Sloane said. "Only the sun was out, and we had those nasty snakkrils to deal with."

My mate generally showed no fear, tending to reminisce and chat when faced with a life-threatening situation. I recalled the trip my friends and I had made through the Quaddrien to reach the remains of the spaceship Doyle had converted into his private compound. The journey had been treacherous, and along the way, we had encountered a nest of the highly venomous snake-like creatures Sloane mentioned.

There had been several solarveyors besides the one we had arrived in back at the compound. It appeared at least one vehicle had survived the blast. If the others had remained unscathed, we faced the possibility of more males coming after us. "Did you happen to see how many males Sarus had working for him?" I asked. Our culture did not train females to be warriors, so I did not believe there would be any in the compound.

"No. I was too busy trying to find the weapons and worrying about saving your gorgeous backside."

"For which I am truly grateful," I said. Human terminology could be confusing. The first time Sloane had referenced my backside, I had misunderstood her meaning and needed clarification. I was pleased to discover that it was me and not a part of my anatomy that had concerned her.

"Good, then you can make it up to me later," she said.

"I intend to." Right after I told her she was my ketiorra and depending on how she reacted to the news.

"If you're planning on getting me something nice, blades are always good." She glanced at me and smiled. "And just so you know, flowers and girly stuff won't work."

I had no idea what girly stuff was and would have to ask Laria and Celeste for an explanation.

"Don't you think if they meant to run us into the ravine, they would've done it already?" Sloane asked. "I'll bet Sarus isn't even on that transport, that he sent those males to bring you back."

"If you are correct, then their goal is to damage the engine," I said, maneuvering around another curve in the road. "It is possible they do not know about you and think that Ryan was the one who helped me. Maybe you should move away from the viewing pane so they cannot see you." Keeping her safe was my primary concern, but I knew she would take offense if I insisted she stay close to me. "It could be used to our advantage later."

"Uh-huh." Sloane sounded skeptical but complied by returning to her seat the same way she had left it.

Another impact to the rear of the vehicle came a few moments later. The engine groaned. The vehicle's lights flickered, and we edged a lot closer to the ravine than I would have liked.

Sloane straightened after being thrown back in her seat. "Okay, so maybe I was wrong. Maybe they are trying to kill us."

I needed to devise a way to stop the other vehicle, and

soon. One or two more hits, and our transport was either going to stop functioning or take us over the side.

Even though the rain was still coming down heavily, I could make out another curve in the road up ahead. As soon as I reached it, the road sloped away from the rocky wall, and the vehicle started to skid. "Hang onto something," I snarled when I felt the jarring impact from the solarveyor behind us. I gripped the controls, trying to keep us from going over the side. Sloane braced her arms on the edge of the control panel in front of her.

The transport continued to slide, my side of the vehicle dipping. Rather than slow it down, I pressed on the accelerator and turned the controls to the right as hard as possible. The engine whined, screeching so loud it grated.

Finally, the transport shuddered, the wheels connected with the hardened surface beneath the layer of slimy mud and swung away from the ravine. The right side bounced against the rock wall several times before I could straighten it out.

The solarveyor behind us had not been so lucky. With our transport no longer in its path, the operator overcompensated his acceleration and drove headlong into the ravine.

The jarring motion had knocked Sloane sideways. She squealed as she tumbled to the floor. "Little one," I called after stopping the vehicle, then jumping to my feet and racing to her side so I could kneel beside her. "Are you all right?" I did not wait for her to answer before running my hands along her arms, checking for injuries.

"Yes, but let's not do that again." She flashed me a forced smile. "With all the bruises I'm going to have, I'll have to make a trip to the city, so I can soak in one of Khyron's fancy bathtubs."

The people that lived in the settlement and the outlying smaller communities did not have the tubs she referenced. They used walk-in stalls for bathing, which were barely big enough to accommodate my larger frame. I helped her to her feet. "Perhaps it would be easier if I built you a bathing tub of your own."

Sloane rubbed her backside, her eyes sparkling with interest. "I have two questions."

"Which are?"

"First, do you even know how to construct a tub? And, second, will I be expected to share it?"

"Yes, I do," I said. "And with me…but only if you wish to." She immediately picked up my insinuation about bathing together. It was the first time I had ever silenced the female with my words or seen her cheeks turn such a bright shade of red.

She was resilient and recovered quickly by changing the subject. "I don't think we'll need to worry about the males in the other transport anymore."

I had to agree. The odds of anyone getting out of the vehicle alive and climbing back up to the road were slim. There were flesh-eating creatures that preferred the darkness and lived at the bottom of ravines. They would ensure anyone who survived the crash would not live much longer.

"Since it does not look like anyone else is following us, I suggest we stop here for the night," I said.

"Sounds like a good idea to me," Sloane said, rolling her shoulders.

"To save power, we will need to shut down the engine," I said, turning back to the control panel. Conserving energy might be moot. The last hit, though not as severe as the previous two, might have caused enough damage to keep us from going anywhere in the morning.

"Then it's a good thing I still have these," Sloane said, reaching inside her pocket and pulling out the bag containing what was left of her zapharite stones. "I'm going to check to see if they stocked any food and if there are any other supplies we can use." She handed me one of the rocks, then held out another one and used it to light her way to the rear of the vehicle.

I would have preferred spending my time admiring the sway of her hips. Shutting down the engine and securing the access panel so no one could enter while we slept was more important.

While I attended my tasks, I could hear her rummaging around inside the storage units. "Oooh, this looks promising," Sloane said.

"You found food?" I asked.

"No, something even better."

She reappeared a few minutes later, carrying numerous blades, which she placed on the bench behind my seat.

I shook my head and groaned. "Only you would find being armed more appealing than eating."

"I'm surprised you lasted this long without wanting to replace your weapon." She glanced at my hip, then picked up a blade similar in length to the one I had lost and handed it to me.

I brushed my fingers along her jaw, catching a few brown strands and tucking them behind her ear. "I had other things on my mind."

***

SLOANE

Showing affection wasn't something Garyck usually did. When he caressed the side of my check, I wondered if maybe he'd hit his head after he'd been stunned and was having some kind of delayed reaction. I rose on my tiptoes and pressed the back of my hand to his forehead. "Are you all right?"

He furrowed his brows and took my hand. "I am fine, but we need to talk."

My concern increased. He was a private male who didn't go out of his way to be social, so having a lengthy conversation wasn't normal for him either.

"Okay," I said, sounding skeptical. "It's going to be a

long night. Do you mind if we get settled first?" It had been hours since I'd eaten. I was tired, hungry, and my body ached. The transport didn't have a heating system, and the rain had made the cold evening temperatures even chillier. If what he had to say wasn't going to be pleasant, then I'd rather hear it while in a semi-comfortable state.

"That would be preferable," he said.

"Great, because there were also some blankets and a glow emitter in the storage unit. I'll be right back." I turned and hurried back to the rear of the vehicle, anxious to know what Garyck wanted to discuss. Our situation wasn't good, but it wasn't dire either, at least not yet.

Knowing him, he'd come up with some plan that involved me staying behind while he went back to Sarus's compound to make sure all the weapons had been destroyed. I was willing to hear what he had to say, but I wasn't leaving his side and was prepared to argue vehemently against it.

When I pulled the blankets out of the upper storage unit, some small packets containing what appeared to be dehydrated meats dropped to the floor. "It looks like there is some food back here after all," I called to Garyck.

It wasn't smart to go anywhere on this planet without packing food and some type of beverage. Most people had containers of water, but mercs usually kept a stash of ale. Whoever was responsible for keeping the transport stocked didn't disappoint me. I looked in the adjacent unit and found several containers of each, which I added to my pile of goods.

The emitter, which reminded me of a flashlight, only brighter, was powered by a combination of zapharite stones and ketaurran solar technology. Now that I had more light, I didn't need to use my stone anymore and returned it to my pocket.

As I stacked everything on top of the blankets, I contemplated sleeping arrangements. When I started imagining my body curled up next to Garyck's, I pushed the thoughts away. It wouldn't do any good to wish for things that weren't meant to be.

After gathering the supplies, I returned to the front and spread a blanket out the walkway floor. Garyck remained silent, but I could feel his intense gaze on me the entire time. I removed my blade and placed it on the nearest bench, along with the emitter, then grabbed two of the meat packets and settled on one end of the blanket. "I'm ready when you are," I said, patting the spot opposite me.

Garyck placed the replacement blade I'd given him next to mine, then returned my stone as he sat down next to me.

After handing him a packet, I opened the one I'd kept for myself and sniffed the contents to make sure they were edible. The dried meat smelled okay, so I stuck a small piece in my mouth and chewed. "Not bad," I said after swallowing. "Not as good as the stuff you make, but it'll do." Garyck did a lot of hunting, cooked whatever he trapped, and always shared it with my friends and me.

I waited for him to eat a few bites, then asked, "What did you want to talk about?"

He briefly stared at his lap as if compiling his thoughts. When he finally raised his head, he said, "I would like to apologize for my recent behavior."

"You mean when you foolishly attacked Sarus and ended up a prisoner? Or when you went out of your way to avoid me back at the settlement?" More than my body was suffering from bruising. My emotions, which included my heart, were still in a raw state, and I had no intention of making this easy for him.

"Both." He took my packet and set it with his on the blanket, then held my gaze, his amber eyes filled with regret and caring. "When I saw Sarus, all I could think about was ending the wretched male's life." He wrapped his hands around mine. "And protecting my ketiorra."

I didn't have a problem understanding or empathizing with the first part of his comment. I'd experienced a similar reaction when I discovered Sarus was still alive. It was the latter part of what he'd said that I struggled with.

Stressful situations could sometimes distort perceptions, so could hopeful thinking. "Ketiorra?" I repeated, more to confirm that I hadn't misunderstood him than anything else.

"Yes, Sloane. You are my mate." He rarely used my real name. I knew he was genuinely serious when he didn't address me with the nickname he'd given me.

I didn't ask him how long he'd known. It had to be soon after we'd met, and he'd gotten a good whiff of my scent. "If you knew all this time, why didn't you say anything?"

Thinking that he'd been disappointed, that I somehow didn't meet his expectations, was the only answer that made any sense. It would also explain his recent avoidance. My chest tightened, and I pulled my hands from his. I forced myself to breathe, my words coming out raspy. "Is it because you didn't want me?"

"No," he growled. "Why would you consider that a possibility?"

I crossed my arms and scowled, anger replacing the hurt. "I don't know, maybe because you've been *avoiding* me."

"And for that, I am truly sorry. I thought if I stayed away, the need to make you mine would subside," he said.

"And did it?" I asked, not sure I wanted to hear the answer.

"No, it made me irritable. Even Zaedon did not like spending time alone with me. He told me I was grumpy and needed to fix whatever was bothering me."

"You, grumpy," I teased. "That's hard to believe."

He snorted, then smiled. Not a barely noticeable rise at the end of his lips, but a full grin that formed dimples.

I pinched his cheek. "Did you know you're rather adorable when you smile?"

"Ketaurran warriors are not adorable," he huffed.

"Cuteness aside, you still haven't explained why you thought it was a good idea to stay away," I said.

The sparkle faded from his eyes, his expression growing somber. "I have been a vryndarr for a very long time. I guarded Khyron's sire before his death." His voice cracked when he spoke of Khyron's father. "I failed my duty to keep him alive."

When he paused, I sensed there was more to his explanation, something that was difficult for him to share. I was afraid if I said anything, he wouldn't continue, so I placed my hand on his leg, offering encouragement.

"I was also captured by Sarus, so I know firsthand what the despicable male is capable of... How he treats his prisoners."

Back at the compound, when Sarus had discussed torturing Garyck in the past with Draejek, it took everything I had to control my anger and remain pressed against the building. If I'd known what Sarus had done to him when I was hiding under the solarveyor, I might have risked gutting the male myself.

"My life as a warrior had always been a solitary one. I never believed I would ever find my mate," he said. "Then I found you, and after everything that happened in my past, I feared that I would not be able to protect you."

He knew me too well, knew I would argue about being able to take care of myself, and held up his hand to stop me. "I could not face losing you after claiming you. The pain would have been unbearable."

I gritted my teeth, and Garyck must have guessed that I was doing my best not to yell at him because he had the nerve to grin.

"I will admit that I do not think clearly where you are concerned," he said. "It has taken me some time to figure out that no matter what the future brings, we are better together than apart." He took my hand again, and this time I didn't pull away. "Please tell me that I have not ruined things between us."

For a male who didn't spend much time socializing, he was quite capable of saying the right thing. My irritation faded, and I tapped my chin while contemplating my answer. It didn't hurt that my hesitation had him visibly squirming. "Well, that depends," I said.

"On what?"

"On whether or not you're going to continue ignoring me," I said. "If you hadn't noticed, talking is good. Or you can keep grunting. Either way works for me."

"Any other requests?" he asked.

"As a matter of fact, there is," I said, crawling onto his lap and straddling his waist. "I still want you to build me a bathing tub." I smirked and shifted my weight, rubbing against his shaft, which immediately hardened. "And I expect you to make it big enough for both of us."

"Little one, I…" he groaned.

"Can I take that as a yes?"

He answered by capturing my mouth with his. His actions were possessive, intoxicating, and left me panting. After releasing me from the kiss, he nuzzled my neck, his breath warming my ear as he spoke. "I recall a threat you made shortly after we met. One that involved removing my hair while I slept." He nipped the side of my throat. "Should I be concerned if you spend the night in my arms?"

I remembered the exchange he'd specified. It was the day after we'd spent a night in an outpost and were getting ready to ride some chaugwai into the Quaddrien. I flashed him a mischievous grin. "Are you worried?"

"Sloane," he growled.

"Do you still have a problem with my height or believe I'll need constant assistance with mounting?" I asked, using the exact words he'd spoken to me back then.

"There is nothing about you that I find unappealing," he said, his voice deeper than usual. "I will be more than happy to assist you with any future mounting."

"We aren't talking about riding a chaugwas anymore,

are we?" I asked.

"No, we are not." He nuzzled my neck again, sending delicious shivers across my skin. "When ketaurrans bond, they do not have an official ceremony?" he said, pulling back so he could see my face. "Do you wish to have a wedding like Celeste's, so you can wear a dress?"

Garyck had been in the gathering room when I'd argued with my friends, so I knew he was well aware of my views on the subject. "No, I do not wish to have a wedding."

"As much as I look forward to seeing you in this garment that frightens you, I will abide by your wishes."

"Thank you," I said. "And, so we're clear. It takes more than a bunch of fabric to scare me."

"I will make a note." He chuckled.

"Now," I said, sucking his earlobe into my mouth and grinning when a rumble rose from his chest. "Are you going to claim me, or should I be retrieving more blankets to make another bed?"

He rolled me onto my back so fast it made me dizzy. After settling his waist between my thighs, he said, "If you agree to our bonding, then I will ensure that you never sleep alone again."

I didn't care that the floor was hard and the blanket didn't provide much insulation. Garyck and I were together, and that was all that mattered. Not to mention, I wanted his naked body pressed against mine. "I can't believe we haven't removed our clothes yet."

"A task that is easily remedied," he said, pushing away from me. He started with my boots. Once they were off, and my dagger was safely set aside, the rest of my clothes came off quickly.

We'd waited so long to be together that neither of us was interested in a leisurely game of teasing and seduction. Slow exploration filled with touching and learning every inch of his body could wait until later. Right now, I longed to be his, to have him ease the growing ache building inside me. The second my skin was bare, I got on my knees to help him strip.

After Garyck's shirt joined my discarded clothes, temptation got the better of me. I skimmed my fingertips across the smooth muscles and soft golden scales covering his chest.

"Little one," he growled, more guttural than usual when my hand found its way to his hardened shaft before he'd finished removing his pants. "If you do not cease what you are doing, I will lose control and not be able to claim you completely."

"I thought the vryndarr oozed self-control," I teased.

"Not when our ketiorras taunt us." He urged me back on the blanket, easing his way between my legs again.

"Are you ready to lose control now?"

"Almost," he said, grinning. He used one hand to pin my wrists, gently yet firmly, above my head and wrapped the end of his tail around my ankle. "Now, I am ready."

"Then, by all means, get on with the claiming," I said, wiggling my hips.

He drove into me hard and deep, the sensation so intense it had me gasping. After that, his movements were steady, each thrust fulfilling my body's needs and pushing me toward an orgasm I knew would be monumental.

Reaching between us and pressing his thumb against my sensitive area was all it took for waves of exquisite pleasure to rip through me. "Garyck," I called out, my body trembling.

He continued to drive in and out, his momentum increasing, his body tensing as he found his release.

Garyck pressed a kiss to my forehead, then collapsed on his side and pulled me into his arms. When our panting subsided, he dragged the additional blanket over our bodies to keep out the chill in the air, which wasn't necessary because his body gave off a lot of warmth.

"Sloane," he said, just as I was drifting off to sleep.

"Yes." I opened my eyes and lifted my head. We hadn't

bothered to turn off the glow emitter, so I could easily see his face.

"I would like you to have this." He rolled on his side and slipped the band from his arm.

The sculpted metal strip was important to him, a treasured possession. The sentiment behind him gifting it to me had my throat constricting. "Are you sure?"

"Yes." He reformed the metal so it would fit around my smaller arm. "I want you to know how important you are to me every time you look at it."

I was so touched by his gesture that I couldn't form words. After returning to his arms, I pulled him into a seductive kiss, then spent my time passionately demonstrating how much I cared about him.

CHAPTER FIFTEEN

GARYCK

I was a light sleeper and was pulled from my comfortable slumber by Sloane, who released a long, drawn-out moan as she stretched beside me. When she skimmed her nails across the scales on my chest, I opened my eyes. "Do you wish to play some more?" I asked. Though we had spent a great deal of the evening exploring each other's bodies, I would not be opposed to doing it again.

"Yes. Always." She grinned mischievously. "But right now, the sun is almost out, and we need to get going."

When she pulled back the blanket and tried to get up, I wrapped the end of my tail around her ankle. "Some males never learn," she giggled as she ran a fingertip along the length.

Shudders rippled along my entire body, and I snatched my tail back. "You do not play fair, little one." I rolled on my side and propped my head on my elbow. I still could not believe that this beautiful female had allowed me to claim her, that we had officially bonded.

"You're just figuring that out?" She rummaged through

the pile of clothes on the floor until she found her pants. She bent over to pull them on and gave me a magnificent view of her backside, which did not help the already hardened state of my shaft.

After slipping into her shirt, Sloane walked over to the bench beneath the viewing pane facing the ravine. She plopped down on the seat and used her fingers to comb through her hair. During one of our later intimate moments, I had removed the leather binding. I wanted to see the silky strands draped over her shoulders similarly to how they were now.

"You know, I've been thinking," she said, dividing the lengths into three semi-equal sections, then twisting them into a single braid.

"Should I be concerned?" I asked.

"Not amused," she said.

"Go on. I'm listening."

"Anyway, neither of us knows our way around this area, and there's a good chance that someone else will come looking for us when the other transport doesn't return. Maybe we should head back." She finished securing the tie, then flipped the braid over her shoulder. "I'm also worried about our friends. They don't know about Sarus, and if he survived the blast, then they could end up in trouble when they reach his compound."

I had been concerned about our friends too. Still, I knew from experience Burke would weigh all options and not risk the dangers that accompanied traveling through a storm at night. Sloane had given our situation a lot of thought and, no doubt, come up with a feasible plan. I had several ideas of my own but was interested to hear what she had to say. I threw back the cover and reached for my pants, grinning when her gaze dropped below my waist.

"We can't discount that Sarus, and most likely Draejek, might decide to come after us themselves. We don't have enough power to make it very far, and we can't risk sitting here and waiting for the solars to charge."

"I agree." I had finished dressing and sat on the bench next to her to pull on my boots. "What do you suggest?"

"I think we should ditch this vehicle…literally," Sloane said.

"Ditch?" Her use of the word meant something I did not understand.

She grinned. "We should drive this transport into the ravine. If someone comes looking for us, maybe they'll keep driving. Worst case scenario, they spot one of the vehicles and assume they both went over the edge during the storm, leaving no survivors. On the downside, it means walking back to the compound."

If someone else came looking for us as Sloane presumed, I doubted they would climb down in the ravine to verify we, or rather I, was dead. I was still going with the assumption that they presumed Ryan was the one to aid my escape.

"It is a good idea and might provide us with additional time to reach the compound."

"Exactly." Sloane got up from the bench and smoothed one of the blankets out on the floor. Next, she walked to the rear of the vehicle, returning a few minutes later with several water containers and food packets, which she placed in the middle of the blanket.

She grabbed the spare blades she had found the night before and the stun stick, then placed them with the other items she had gathered. When she noticed that I was watching, I quirked a brow, and she answered, "I couldn't find any travel bags in the storage units, and we'll need supplies."

"We will be climbing, so you might want to leave anything that is not necessary behind," I said.

"Climbing? Why?" Sloane straightened and frowned.

My mate was daring, but scaling rocks was not something she enjoyed doing. "We cannot use the road and will need to travel along the top of the ledge to stay out of sight." I stood and hooked the sheathed blade she had given me to my belt.

"Oh, I hadn't thought about that." She knelt to pull the ends of the blanket together and secured them in a knot. She hadn't added anything new to the pile, but she hadn't removed any of the items she had already placed on top of it either.

"If you are concerned about falling, I will be more than happy to protect your backside." I chuckled, thankful her hands were empty. Otherwise, I was certain she would have thrown something at me.

"I'm sure I can make the climb by myself, but if it's my backside you're interested in, I might let you play with it later."

Sloane did not have a problem speaking her mind. It appeared anything to do with our bonding had been included in her list of topics. It was rare that anything she said could bring heat to my cheeks, but she had managed to do so anyway.

"Are you ready?" she asked, then snagged the makeshift bundle off the floor and tossed it over her shoulder.

I wanted to tell her no because after our bout of playful banter, all I wanted to do was take her back to bed, not make a long trek to the compound. Reluctantly, I nodded, then waited for her to open the access panel. When I noticed that the soil covering the ground was still damp, I placed a hand on her arm to stop her from exiting.

"The transport is heavy and will make tracks in the dirt. If we want anyone who shows up to believe we went into the ravine along with it, then we cannot leave any footprints."

When I parked the solarveyor, it was close to the rock wall, not the ravine. Unfortunately, the gap was too wide for Sloane to jump across easily. "Can you make it to the boulders, or would you like some assistance?"

"Seriously," she said, rolling her eyes, then taking several steps backward. Sloane hurried past me and, in a smooth, graceful movement, leaped through the opening and landed on the nearest boulder. She grinned and readjusted the bag. "Just waiting for you."

My mate's determination, though sometimes frustrating, was impressive. I had seen her face similar obstacles before, and she never failed to astonish me. "So I see," I said, walking over to the control panel.

The way the engine sputtered and whined confirmed that it had received a great deal of damage. It also reinforced Sloane's suggestion that destroying the solarveyor was our best option.

It took me a few minutes to bring the transport to life, then rig it to move. The vehicle's motions were slow and jerky, giving me plenty of time to exit before it reached its destination. After jumping onto a flattened, rocky surface a few feet away from Sloane, I watched the transport roll over the edge, the metal hull scraping against rock before crashing into the darkened depths below.

I took the blanket bag from Sloane and slung it over my shoulder. During my training to become a vryndarr, I had scaled numerous rock walls, sometimes limited to using one hand. Transporting the extra weight would not burden me the way it would her. "Shall we," I said, motioning for her to climb ahead of me.

"I could've carried it myself," she grumbled.

Sloane was indeed a warrior and not the type of female who asked others to do what she could do herself. "I know," I said, not wanting her to think I considered her weak.

We were headed into another perilous situation that could result in our deaths. Once we started moving, we climbed in silence. It was difficult not to stare at Sloane's backside and wish we could spend more time in each other's arms. I concentrated on ensuring that she made it to the top safely and listened for the possible approach of another solarveyor. The blast may have destroyed the laser weapons, but after being attacked by the other transport, I did not believe Sarus had lost many of his followers, if any.

Now that the sun was out and the clouds that caused the previous night's rainfall had dissipated, traveling would be easier. Some storms appeared without warning. Using the top of the rocky ledge to make our way back to the compound would aid in hiding from Sarus's males. It would not shelter us if the weather changed dramatically.

Once we reached the top, I took a moment to survey the landscape in all directions. From where I was standing, the rock formations on either side of the road below seemed to stretch in both directions for a long distance. There were no obvious signs of any communities or cities in the direction we had been heading. Returning to the compound had been a wise choice.

Sloane held a hand over her eyes to block out the sunlight and studied the direction we were heading. "Any idea where we are or how far we traveled last night?" she asked after shifting her blue gaze to me.

"I am not familiar with our surroundings. I have never traveled past the Quaddrien."

"So, new territory for both of us," she said, then pointed. "I assume that dark line curving its way through the rocks is the road, and if we follow it, we'll eventually end up at the compound."

"Yes, that is the goal," I said.

She puffed out an exasperated breath. "Not a five-minute walk then."

"No, most assuredly not." I was good at determining distances. I had spent most of my time concentrating on the storm and keeping us alive to calculate how far we had traveled.

"Then we'd better get going. I'd rather not be stuck up on these rocks all day."

CHAPTER SIXTEEN

SLOANE

I estimated that Garyck and I had hiked for an hour, maybe a little longer. The boulders and hard-packed dirt that I walked on were a light tan and produced a bright glare. I'd been squinting for so long that the muscles around my eyes were starting to ache.

The temperature had risen, but it wasn't bad yet. Without any clouds or plant life to block out the sun's rays, the heat would eventually reach an uncomfortable level.

My stomach picked that instance to rumble and reminded me that I hadn't eaten anything after getting up to start the day.

"Maybe we should take a break." Garyck glanced at my midsection and grinned.

I loved seeing him smile, something he'd done more since telling me I was his ketiorra than he had in all the time I'd known him.

"Maybe a spot out of the sun." He pressed a fingertip to my arm. My skin had already gained a soft pink hue and left a white impression where he touched me. I wasn't looking forward to the burn I'd have to deal with later. It was one of those times when I envied the protective layer of soft golden scales Garyck had on his arms and chest.

"That spot should work," Garyck said, lifting his chin toward a patch of shade near a small outcropping.

There were very few creatures living on Ketaurrios that I liked. The worst of them lived in the sandy and rocky terrains. Crognats were my least favorite. The tiny pale gold creatures looked like a cross between a beetle and a lizard and stung anyone who got close to them. They also liked cool, dark places.

I pulled out my knife and crouched near the ground, using the tip to poke any loose dirt or crevices near the rocky base where one of the creatures might be hiding. After checking the entire area twice, I put my blade away. "Okay, I think we're good," I said after taking a seat on the ground and patting the place next to me.

Garyck chuckled as he sat down beside me. "Are you sure you would not like to check it one more time?"

"Hey, crognats are devious, so as far as I'm concerned, you can never be too careful," I said, nudging his shoulder. "Besides, isn't it a ketiorra's responsibility to look after her mate, even if he unwisely gets himself bitten?" Not that I ever needed a reason to look out for his safety. "And as much as I enjoy touching your gorgeous body, I'd rather the reason be something other than applying ointment to a critter bite."

"Little one," Garyck warned, his discomfort noticeably obvious when he used the blanket bundle to cover his lap.

Satisfied that I'd won that round of exchanging barbs, I reached over and untied the blanket's knot, then handed him a water container before grabbing one for myself.

After taking a long, much-needed swallow, I snagged a piece of meat from the packet he held out to me. Once I'd finished that piece and reached for another, a thought occurred to me, and I asked, "Don't you think it's strange that we haven't seen any signs of another solarveyor yet?"

Sarus hadn't known that I'd been in the compound, so he must have concluded that Garyck was the one who'd destroyed his new weapons. I still believed that, because of their location, more than one transport had made it through the explosion unscathed. Sarus was ruthless. There was no way he'd let Garyck escape punishment or even death.

"Yes," he said. "It is troubling."

When he continued to stare at the horizon, I followed the direction of his gaze and noticed that several clouds had formed in the distance. I didn't think the lack of another solarveyor was the only thing he was concerned about. A similar sight back on Earth wasn't anything to worry about, but on this planet, dismissing any formation in the sky was a mistake.

We wouldn't have any protection if it started to rain. I hadn't seen any caves. If there were any nearby, they'd be closer to the base of the rock formations. They'd take time to find. Time we didn't have.

"I think we should get going," he said, placing the empty meat packet and my half-drained water container back on the blanket before securing the knot.

"No arguments from me," I said. I couldn't wait to get out of the heat, but complaining about it wouldn't change anything. "The sooner we get to the compound and verify that all the weapons were destroyed, the sooner we can head home."

I missed Laria and Celeste. The mission hadn't seemed the same without them. I also couldn't wait to tell them about Garyck and me. Though I was certain they'd figure it out as soon as they saw us together.

"I'd like to reach the compound before Burke and the others," I said. I was worried about my other teammates. Escaping last night had been a priority, but not at the risk of something terrible happening to my friends. They'd faced the same disadvantages Garyck and I had with the storm but could move much faster with their transport than we could on foot.

There was also the possibility that they didn't find my trail of zapharite stones. Even so, desolate areas like this one didn't have a lot of alternative driving routes. My friends were smart and would eventually find the road leading to the compound...and Sarus.

"Me too," Garyck said, his tone laced with a similar concern. Because of our height differences, his strides were usually longer than mine. Up until now, he'd kept them shorter to remain by my side. Thinking about what could happen if we didn't get there soon had ramped up my anxiety, and I didn't mind increasing my pace to keep up with him.

Part of the trail we'd taken had included inclines. After walking a little further, the downward slope became more noticeable. "Do you think we're getting closer?" I asked.

"Yes, I believe the compound is past that lower ridge over there," Garyck said. He pointed at an area up ahead where the rocky wall on the other side of the road angled closer to the ground.

Our trail ended approximately half an hour later and turned into a tapered drop-off. Most rocky areas on the planet were never lacking when it came to boulders. Garyck and I crouched next to the three stacked side-by-side near the edge of the rock wall running beside the road below.

We were close enough to see the compound, but things were a little blurry from this distance. "I wish I'd thought to grab Burke's binoculars before I left," I said. "They'd sure come in handy right about now."

If we'd been up higher, I might have been able to see the entire layout. From where we were, I could only see a couple of buildings and none of the solarveyors. "I don't see any movement, do you?"

Garyck glanced at me and furrowed his brows. "No, and I do not like it."

CHAPTER SEVENTEEN

GARYCK

Dread skittered across every scale on my body. I did not like being out in the open but had no choice. The distance between the last of the rock formation and the nearest building in the compound did not provide anything that Sloane and I could use to remain hidden.

Sarus was treacherous and not to be underestimated. Thoughts of the old drezdarr filled my mind. The guilt associated with his loss was a painful reminder of the past. Confirming the laser weapons had been destroyed was only part of my plan when I agreed to return with Sloane. Making sure Sarus took his last breath, and would no longer be a threat to Khyron or anyone else I cared about, was my ultimate goal.

Draejek needed to be eliminated as well. It was evident that the male possessed leadership qualities. He had supported Sarus's cause, and I did not trust that he would walk away. The blaster he possessed would also have to be dismantled. It might not be able to start a war, but one shot from a distance could end a life. It had the potential of causing chaos and changing the unity our team had been striving to achieve.

My priority, above all else, was protecting my ketiorra. Now that Sloane and I had bonded, my instincts were more intense, and I struggled not to sling her over my shoulder and take her someplace safe.

When I had first met the female warriors, it had taken some time to adjust to Sloane's warrior side. I might disapprove of her daring risks, but I admired and respected that part of her and would never do anything to hinder or change it. So, instead of reacting emotionally, I took her hand to keep her by my side as we ran.

Once we reached the end of the first building, I glanced along the side to see if Sarus had stationed any of his males outside. When I saw none, I worked my way along the exterior, with Sloane following closely behind me. The wall had several panes; all shuttered to block out the sunlight. I moved until I reached the first one, then strained to listen for any movement inside, and I didn't hear any noise.

The longer I went without seeing or hearing anyone else, the more anxious I became. After the havoc Sloane had created the night before, it made no sense that there would not be any guards posted anywhere.

I fingered the hilt of my blade and continued forward, crouching as I crept beneath the panes. Much to my frustration, Sloane slipped in front of me and peered around the corner. The open area in front of all the structures was empty. Even the solarveyors were gone.

She straightened and, in a lowered voice, asked, "Where is everyone?"

"I do not know," I said, the situation perplexing and making me even more wary.

"Do you think Sarus and the others abandoned the place?" She took a few hesitant steps away from the building. "And if he did, do you think they'll be coming back?"

"Sarus has always been a controlling and greedy individual," I said. "He is also a strategist and may have had a backup plan." A plan he must have initiated when the males he sent to presumably retrieve me had not returned.

"It will make it a little hard to get home without transportation," Sloane said. "I'm beginning to think we made a mistake when we ran our solarveyor into the ravine."

I did not want her to second guess her proposal, and I placed my hand on her arm. "We would not have gotten far. There was too much damage."

"Until we can come up with a way to get out of here that doesn't involve walking back to the settlement, I say we take a look at the building that contained the weapons."

"We should check the other dwellings first," I said.

"Okay, you can start with this one." She smacked the building we were standing beside. "I'll check the one over there." Sloane lifted her chin toward the first one on her right.

"Perhaps we should inspect them together." Any other time, I would not have a problem searching separately. I could not get rid of the feeling that we had somehow walked into a trap and would not relax until I verified that we were indeed alone.

Sloane slapped her hands on her hips. "I don't think that's necessary. I can take care—,"

The rumble of an engine echoing in the distance put an end to her argument. I slipped my arm around her waist and pulled her back into the shadows. We had a direct line of sight to the approaching vehicle, which meant whoever was inside would be able to see us as soon as they arrived. "We cannot stay here," I said, motioning to the rear of the building Sloane had planned to investigate.

She followed me as I hurried to the opposite side of the structure where we could get a better view of the new arrivals. It also brought us closer to what was left of a building. A portion of the roof had collapsed. Part of the exterior wall closest to us was missing. Some of the boards, charred and in pieces, were scattered on the ground.

If the explosion had resulted in a fire, the rain most likely aided in putting it out. Even after hours of sunlight, the shaded areas near any of the buildings should have shown signs of moisture. They appeared to be dry, so I did not think the compound had received the same amount of rain Sloane and I had driven through.

There were also no bodies lying around. Either there were no casualties, or they had already been removed.

"That worked better than I thought," Sloane exclaimed after pausing to observe the devastation. "Though I still think we should check inside to make sure everything was destroyed."

"Later," I said, pulling her back against my body. "After we take care of whoever is in the transport."

***

SLOANE

I didn't mind the possessive way Garyck had pulled me against his chest to keep me from being seen by the approaching solarveyor. He'd growled, his version of scolding, at me enough times since we'd met for me to know that he didn't always approve of some of the risks I took.

I was impressed at how well he controlled his overprotective nature and treated me like any other warrior on the team when facing dangerous opponents. Using the word "we" and not issuing an order for me to stay behind while he handled whoever was in the transport had earned him additional points.

Even though the corner of the building concealed our presence, I still had a good view of the approaching vehicle. My immediate response to impending danger was to draw my blade, but having Garyck's arm wrapped around my midsection, prevented me from reaching it.

Once the transport got closer and was no longer a shiny blur kicking up a trail of dust, I recognized the familiar markings on the exterior hull and relaxed against Garyck's chest.

He loosened his grip. "That is Burke's solarveyor," he said, sounding as relieved as I felt.

The vehicle pulled past the debris littering the ground before parking. Cara was the first to jump out, her short chestnut curls bouncing as she walked over to what was left of the building that housed the weapons. "I think we're in the right place." She bent to examine one of the boards, then smiled as she straightened. "This looks like Sloane's handiwork."

I didn't need compliments to feel good about myself, but hearing the admiration in my friend's voice sent an excited thrill rippling through my system. Her comment about being in the right place also confirmed my suspicions about the storm wiping out part of the stone trail I'd left for them.

"Yes, it does," Burke said, smirking after he and Zaedon joined her.

"But where are they?" Zaedon asked, his alert gaze scanning the compound.

"Right here," I said, strolling in their direction with Garyck pacing a few steps behind me. "Great rescue mission, guys," I said teasingly, though I was glad they hadn't shown up sooner. Every instinct I possessed continued to remind me that Sarus was alive, and I was thankful that my friends hadn't crossed his path before I could warn them.

"We would've arrived sooner if Burke hadn't gotten us lost," Cara said, flashing a wink that only Garyck and I could see.

"I did not get lost," Burke grumbled. "We came across a fork in the road." He shot a sidelong glare at Zaedon. "I was given bad advice on which way to go."

"We ended up in another closed-off area," Cara said. "The roads got worse, and we didn't want to drain the solars, so we decided to wait out the storm."

"Yes, and it didn't hurt that there was plenty of Nayea's ale in one of the storage units," Zaedon said.

"And an extra container of pytiennas," Cara said, scowling at her mate. "Which, of course, someone wasn't willing to share."

She didn't have to mention names. We all knew about Zaedon's flat cake obsession.

Zaedon shrugged, his gaze dropping to the band on my arm. He released an exaggerated sigh. "Finally."

"Finally, what?" Cara asked, then said, "Oh," after noticing the same thing Zaedon had. She pulled me into a hug. "Congratulations." To Garyck, she said, "I hope this means we won't have to put up with any more of your grumpiness."

"I have no idea what you are talking about," Garyck said, slipping his arm along the back of my waist, the warmth welcoming.

Most people were intimidated by Garyck's less than social behavior, or they ignored it. My friends fell in the latter group, so he must have been overly irritable if they'd noticed a change in his demeanor. Knowing I'd been the source of his frustration brought amusement to my lips.

"It appears that Burke getting lost was advantageous," Zaedon said.

Burke rolled his eyes. "I already told you I—"

"Sooo," I interjected before another exchange could ensue. "While you weren't getting lost, did you happen to see any other roads leading out of here?" I asked, still unconvinced that Sarus and the other males had abandoned the compound.

"Not really," Burke said. "There were a couple of gaps in the rocks that looked like they were wide enough for a transport, but I wasn't checking to see if they'd been used recently."

"We also passed a forest area, but the trail leading inside didn't look like anyone had tried driving through it in a long time," Cara said.

A nearby forest explained where Sarus got the wood for his buildings. Garyck and I had been too busy to explore this area thoroughly. If it was littered with numerous trails, there might be more than one way to access the forest. A wooded area or a hidden canyon would be the perfect place to hide several vehicles.

"Where is Des?" Garyck asked. "Did something happen to him?"

I'd been so focused on figuring out what happened to Sarus that I hadn't realized our team was one person short.

"I sent him back to the settlement to give Khyron an update on what you two were doing and to let him know about the bodies," Burke said.

"What bodies?" I asked.

"Ryan and his mysterious friend killed Everett and the other mercs," Cara said.

I'd already overheard Draejek tell Sarus what he'd done, so the news wasn't surprising.

"We learned that Draejek is the name of the male who accompanied Ryan," Garyck said.

"Where is Ryan?" Burke asked, glancing around as if it was the first he'd realized we were the only ones in the compound.

"I'm afraid he's dead," I hitched a thumb over my shoulder. "He's probably underneath that rubble somewhere."

"Is Draejek in there as well?" Zaedon asked.

"We got back here shortly before you did, so we have no idea where he, Sarus, or any of the others went," I said.

"Sarus was here?" Zaedon's dark turquoise eyes widened, and his smile faded. He fisted his hands against his thighs and glared at Garyck. "And you let him live?"

The hand Garyck had pressed to the small of my back

stiffened. He already carried around enough guilt associated with Sarus's actions. I wasn't about to let anyone make him feel worse or have him explain what might be misconstrued as a failed attempt. Even if that someone was one of his closest friends.

"We found ourselves in a difficult situation and decided that destroying the weapons should come first." I took a step forward, not caring if it appeared intimidating. "We were going to double-check that none of them were operational right before you arrived."

"Hold on," Burke said. "Didn't you say you got back here not long before we did? Where did you go?"

"It's a long story," I said. "One I'd be happy to tell you, but later." Of course, the private conversation Garyck and I had shared, along with the details about our intimate time together, would be omitted in the retelling.

"It sounds like there's a lot more we need to know," Cara said, placing a calming hand on Zaedon's arm. I could always count on her to be diplomatic during intense situations. "I'd rather hear it after checking on the weapons and getting out of here." She gave our surroundings a wary glance. "There's something about this place that's unsettling."

I trusted Cara's instincts, sometimes even more than my own. It was definitely time to go if the compound gave her bad vibes. "I agree," I said, stepping over several boards on my way to what was left of the building.

A blast zinged through the air and hit the ground near my feet with enough force to toss dirt into the air. Burke had years of military training and reacted before the rest of us. "Take cover!" he yelled as he dove behind the transport.

Cara had been walking next to me and hurried to reach the partial wall I was rushing toward. Garyck and Zaedon had been too far away and were forced to find protection behind the nearest building.

They were both yelling our names at the same time.

"Were fine," I called, then turned to my friend, who was more angry than afraid of what had happened. If the person hadn't used a weapon that could rip through flesh, she'd already be tearing after them. And I'd be right behind her. "Did you see where the shot came from?" I asked.

"Based on the fact that it missed you and hit the ground, I'd say someone is shooting at us from that roof over there."

I glanced down at my boot and noticed that the shooter hadn't missed, not exactly anyway. "Err. Look what he did to my favorite pair of pants," I groaned and fingered the scorch mark on the fabric. Another half-inch to the left, and he would've gotten my ankle. "It has to be Draejek." I shot a narrow-eyed glare at the structure Cara had suggested. "He does not get to live after this."

"Let's hope he's the only one who has a blaster."

"I checked all the weapons containers before making them go boom, and only one was missing," I said. "So unless there are some containers we don't know about, I'm sure he has the only one."

"Do you think Sarus is up there with him?" Cara asked. She tried to get a better look by peering through a crack between the boards rather than poking her head out and possibly getting shot.

"Either that or he and the other males are hiding somewhere nearby."

"Any idea how many males Sarus had working for him?" Cara asked.

"I only saw a handful when I was stuck under the solarveyor." She raised a brow, and I knew I'd have to explain in detail later. "I was too busy trying to get to the weapons and didn't take the time to check out the other buildings."

"Let's hope it's not a small army then."

Even if we were outnumbered, we stood a better chance of winning when our opponents were armed with blades. The laser weapon reduced our odds considerably.

Several more blasts filled the air seconds before Burke dove and hit the ground next to me. "What the draeck, Burke?" I asked. "Are you trying to get yourself killed?"

No," he said, pushing himself off the ground to sit with his back braced against the wood. "I wanted to see how many blasters we were up against." He grinned. "It looks like there's only the one."

"I'm glad you're happy," Cara said, then punched him in the arm. "But next time, could you find an easier way to get your answer."

Instead of punching Burke too, I joined Cara in glaring and scowling.

I hoped we got out of this alive, and there wouldn't be a next time. "Do you think he plans to keep us trapped here for the rest of the day?" I asked.

"Actually, I'd be okay with that," Burke said. "He'll have difficulty seeing us once the sun goes down."

"There's no way Garyck and Zaedon will wait that long before trying to do something," Cara said. She looked in their direction to make sure they hadn't already moved.

I hated that Garyck and I had been separated and knew his protective instincts would be worse than mine. I risked shifting slightly to peer past Cara. When amber eyes filled with anger met mine, I shook my head, hoping he'd honor my request and not do something that might end his life.

Apparently, Cara didn't want to sit back and wait for the males to try something heroic any more than I did. "Do you think one of you could hit Draejek if I got him to expose more of his body?" she asked, referring to our knife-throwing abilities.

"Maybe, but it's too risky," I said before Burke had a chance to agree. Getting Draejek to show himself meant Cara would have to move out into the open. It was even crazier than Burke's dash from the transport. It was too bad the blanket bundle I'd filled with extra blades had ended up with Garyck. Otherwise, I'd toss them onto the roof. Even if I didn't hit Draejek, it might startle him enough to move.

Luckily, depending on a person's point of view, the decision was taken away from us when Sarus and at least ten more males poured out of two of the buildings opposite us.

CHAPTER EIGHTEEN

GARYCK

It was always reassuring to know my instincts had not failed me, but the instant the laser blast landed in the dirt near Sloane's feet, I wished I had been wrong. I wished I had listened to the warning in my head telling me we had walked into a trap. I wished I had taken her back to the rocky terrain where we could have found shelter and a place to hide.

Instead, my heart had nearly exploded from my chest when I saw how close I had come to losing her and not being able to do anything about it.

My anxiety had lessened, replaced by rage and the need to pummel the male who had threatened my ketiorra. It had gotten worse when Sarus and his males emerged from two of the buildings, one of them the structure Sloane was about to enter before our friends had arrived.

There were no humans among the males who spread out behind Sarus, only ketaurrans. They had each prepared for battle by securing their shoulder-length hair at the nape and attaching at least one blade within easy reach of their hips.

Those human males who had assisted Ryan in relocating the weapons containers shortly after Sloane and I had arrived at the compound were not present. Either they had been the ones who moved the solarveyors, or Sarus had ordered someone to get rid of them the way he had the mercs at the outpost.

Given our current predicament, my plan to find a way to the rooftop so I could disarm Draejek was no longer necessary. Getting to my mate and keeping her alive was all I cared about.

"Surrender now," Sarus said. "Or I will have Draejek shoot you one at a time, starting with the females." He signaled for the male on the roof to come down and join him.

"How do we know if we do as you ask, that you won't shoot us anyway?" Burke called from his hiding spot with Sloane and Cara.

"You have my word," Sarus said.

"You betrayed your sibling, so your word means nothing to me," I said, moving away from the building and making myself an easy target. I did not want to appear overly threatening, so I left Sloane's blanket bundle on the ground next to Zaedon.

Sarus pursed his lips, and if his tail could still move on its own, it would be twitching. Challenging him was unwise, but I would do anything to draw his attention away from the females, from my ketiorra.

"My sibling was weak," Sarus said, distastefully spitting out the words.

"The old drezdarr was not weak," I said. "He understood the value of life. How sharing and collaborating would make us stronger."

"Allowing another species to live on our planet was a reckless decision and further demonstrated his incompetence to be a leader."

"Geez," Sloane said. "It's not like overcrowding was ever an issue."

Right or wrong, Sarus believed in his cause and would dispense with anyone who got in his way. I did not want my mate to be someone he considered a threat. "Little one," I growled, inching closer to her. "Do not provoke him."

"Fine," she groaned.

Sarus had obviously put some thought into his trap. Since he had not sent another transport to search for us, I wondered how he knew Sloane and I would return. "With the weapons gone, why are you still here?" I asked.

"Because Khyron is so predictable," Sarus said, sneering. "I knew he would send others to look for you. Though I am disappointed that he did not come himself." He scratched his jaw. "You showing up here was a surprise. When the males I ordered to bring you back did not return, I assumed they had not survived, and you were on your way back to the settlement."

"You can find your males at the bottom of a ravine," I reported happily.

"Speaking of finding things. We discovered Ryan's body inside the building, underneath some debris," Sarus said. "I take it he is not the one who assisted with your escape."

His summation was correct, so I did not bother answering. I was more interested in learning what else they found when searching through the rubble. If Draejek was the only one armed with a laser blaster, then there was a good chance that none of the other weapons had survived the explosion and ensuing fire.

"No, that would be me," Sloane said, walking over to stand next to me.

I was about to scold her for not staying where she was until I realized she had no choice. Cara and Burke appeared with Draejek walking behind them; his weapon leveled at their backs.

At least Sloane had been smart enough not to tell Sarus she had been the one to destroy his weapons. It would have infuriated the male and reminded him how much he hated humans. During the war, he had demonstrated that being a female did not matter. I feared that if she angered him too much, he would take her life out of spite.

Sarus glanced at the building I had been using for cover and said, "You might as well join your friends, Zaedon."

Zaedon shared a disappointed look with me as he walked toward us. It seemed we were both hoping his presence had been forgotten. He continued past me, not stopping until he had positioned himself between Cara and Draejek. He would do whatever was necessary to protect his ketiorra as I would mine. Even if it meant the risk of being shot by a deadly laser blast.

"With your weapons gone and Khyron not here, what are you planning to do now?" Burke asked Sarus. The male had good leadership abilities, and understanding his enemy's objectives was one of them.

The way Sarus eyed Burke as if he was a lower lifeform and not worth his time made me think he would ignore the question. Sarus's egotistical nature took over. He puffed out his chest and paced a few steps before speaking.

"Khyron cares a great deal about the males who protect him." He turned and looked directly at Zaedon and me. "I wonder if he would trade his life for theirs."

Smug expressions appeared on the faces of the males standing behind Sarus. They knew as well as I did that the answer was "yes."

Sarus returned his attention to Burke. "Unfortunately for you, the vryndarr and their ketiorras will be all the leverage I need." He shifted his gaze to Draejek. "If you wouldn't mind, I would like you to dispose of this human."

Instead of trying to move out of the weapon's range, Burke remained stationary and yelled, "Now, Celeste!"

***

SLOANE

Sarus hated humans. The only reason I could think of for him not to have Draejek shoot Cara and me along with Burke was that he needed leverage to control Garyck and Zaedon. Threatening us would keep both males compliant.

After hearing Sarus order my friend and mentor to death, helplessness washed over me, and all I could do was gape. I couldn't believe Burke was standing there, willing to accept his fate without a fight.

I was even more shocked when I heard him yell Celeste's name. A few seconds later, his odd behavior made sense when my friend stepped out from behind the solarveyor. My mind barely registered her appearance before the silver glint of her knife flew through the air and sliced into the wrist of the hand Draejek was using to hold the laser blaster.

Celeste was better than all of us when it came to wielding blades. Burke could sometimes be a pain in the backside, but he'd earned a great deal more of my admiration. It took a lot of guts and a significant amount of trust for him to hold still rather than duck for cover, so Celeste would have a non-moving target.

The next few minutes were filled with chaos. Draejek screamed and dropped his weapon, then used his free hand to pull out the dagger and toss it to the ground, so he could grip his wrist and try to stop the bleeding. He would lose mobility in his hand if the blade severed tendons and nerves, which it most likely had.

Burke picked up the discarded blaster and Celeste's blade, ensuring that Draejek remained weaponless. Celeste had come armed with an additional knife, which was already out of its sheath. Khyron, Jardun, and Laria spilled out of the transport, blades drawn. The rest of us didn't need an invitation to pull out our blades and join our friends.

We all fanned out, forming a semicircle around Sarus and his group of males with Khyron in the center facing off with his uncle. All the males had drawn their blades; their hardened glares focused on our group as they awaited Sarus's orders.

"Khyron," Sarus hissed. "It appears I underestimated you."

"So it seems," Khyron said, exuding calm, his voice devoid of any emotions, including the anger I knew he had to be feeling.

After everything that Sarus had done, I was impressed at how well Khyron was handling their encounter.

"There will be no bargaining the lives of my vryndarr or any other inhabitants…ever." Khyron emphasized the last of his statement by purposely glaring at each of the males, saving Sarus for last.

"Are you here to seek retribution for your sire's death?" Sarus asked. He gripped the hilt of his blade tighter and curled the fingers of his free hand into a fist.

"I am here to end this once and for all," Khyron said. "If you are determined to rule, you will fight me and me alone for the honor."

"Do you guarantee that no one will interfere?" Sarus asked.

Khyron glanced first to our team members standing to his left, then to those on his right. "No one will interfere." It may have sounded like a statement, but we all knew it was an order we would obey.

He hadn't bothered to ask for the same reassurances from Sarus regarding his males. It hadn't been necessary since Burke was standing off to the side with the laser blaster aimed in their general direction.

Sarus smirked. "And when I win, I will expect the vryndarr to obey me." His arrogance was appalling, and so were the grunts and snorts from the males who found his comment amusing.

"Trust is earned, so that is one thing I cannot

guarantee," Khyron said.

Khyron losing was a possibility I refused to ponder. A world without the current drezdarr would be a world of tyranny. With Sarus's vehement views about humans, it would also mean the extinction of our race on the planet.

"Khyron, you can't," Celeste said, placing a hand on his arm. My friend could lose her mate, and her plea tore at my heart, making it hard to swallow.

"It will be all right, zadierra," Khyron said, reassuring her with the affectionate term that translated into treasured one in his language.

The tension radiating from Garyck, Jardun, and Zaedon was so thick that I expected them to voice similar objections. They were loyal to the drezdarr and would support his decision, even if it meant his death. I wouldn't be surprised if one or all of them offered to take Khyron's place in the upcoming battle.

"Shall we get started?" Sarus asked, then added a condescending taunt. "Unless you need more time to console your female."

I had my own reasons for hating Sarus and was willing to push them aside and let Khyron handle things. Going after one of my best friends was more than I could stand. "One more wisecrack like that, and you and your male parts will require consoling." I stepped forward only to have Garyck pull me back against his firm chest. "Sloane, please," he whispered into my ear. "It has to be this way if we want the collaboration to succeed."

Having Garyck remind me that there was more at stake than Sarus's insults was annoying. He might be right, but it didn't mean I had to like it. "Fine." I patted his arm so he'd release me. Once he did, I couldn't help tossing out an insult of my own. "The miserable piece of chaugwas excrement better stick to the honor thing, or I'll personally give him a taste of my new blade."

Khyron hadn't taken his pale blue eyes off Sarus since I'd threatened the other male's manhood. He pretended to ignore my comment, but I'd glimpsed a slight upturn to the ends of his lips.

"Female, your threats are insignificant," Sarus said. I'd expected him to get angry and proclaim my impending death or something similar, not dismiss me with a flip of his wrist.

To Khyron, he said, "We are wasting time."

"I think we should see to Draejek's injuries first," Celeste said. I didn't think stalling the inevitable motivated my friend's request. She wasn't a callous person, and if she'd wanted Draejek dead, she could have easily ended his life rather than disarming him with her knife.

Sarus shrugged as if Draejek's life was meaningless now that he was no longer useful. He didn't make a move to help him, nor did he order any of the other males to provide assistance.

As much as I wanted Draejek to suffer for his role in supporting Sarus, I couldn't stand by and watch him slowly bleed to death. "I'll do it," I said, then slipped away from the group and headed for the transport.

It didn't take me long to find a medical kit from a storage unit and step back outside. Garyck was where I'd left him, his attention split between watching Khyron and me. I smiled to let my mate know that I understood his need to protect the drezdarr was important and that I'd be careful before hurrying over to Draejek.

The male had removed his belt and tightened it around his arm above the injury. His face had paled, and he was leaning against the wall of the nearest building as if he might topple over any second.

I approached Draejek slowly, aware that he was as wary of my movements as I was of his. After stopping a few feet away, I set the kit on the ground. "Do you mind if I take a look," I said, holding out my hand.

Draejek jerked away from me. "Do not touch me, female. Humans are treacherous creatures and cannot be trusted."

"Of all the ungrateful..." I mumbled. "Do you really want to get into a discussion about treachery?" I slapped my hands on my hips. "Or do you want me to take care of your wound before you bleed out and die?"

"If it were me, I would let her help," Garyck said as he walked up behind me. Having him close and hearing his supportive tone warmed me to the core. "You do not look like you will be able to stay standing much longer."

Draejek angrily swished his tail, the movement a little sluggish. "All right," he grumbled, then slowly sank to the ground.

Draejek, Garyck, and I weren't that far from the others, so we'd be able to hear any additional conversing, but no one spoke. An eerie silence filled the air as everyone waited for me to finish. I hurried to open the kit and extract some bandages and the special healing cream that Vurell had concocted from a plant that grew near the settlement.

I didn't have the medical training necessary to repair Draejek's wound properly. But I'd had plenty of experience applying cream and bandages to stop the bleeding until we returned home. Now that Draejek was cooperating, addressing his injury went faster than expected. I didn't want him to misinterpret what I planned to do next and said, "I need to remove the belt and make sure that the bleeding doesn't start again."

He nodded, then straightened his arm for me. I smiled, glad when no red seeped through the thick layers I'd wrapped around his wrist. "That should hold until we can get you to a physician," I said, packing up the kit, then getting to my feet.

Knowing he disliked humans, I wasn't expecting any thanks from Draejek. I was surprised to hear the words and see a flicker of appreciation in his eyes.

I wasn't in a hurry to see Sarus and Khyron fight, but the older male's patience wouldn't last much longer. I placed the kit on the floor inside the transport and took my place next to Garyck with our friends.

Whatever happened next was going to change our futures forever. I inhaled a deep breath, hoping that the outcome would be a good one.

CHAPTER NINETEEN

GARYCK

Even though Sloane gave me a look to let me know she would be all right, I was not comfortable leaving her alone with Draejek and had followed her. Sarus might be devious and lack integrity, but I did not think he would try to attack Khyron and Celeste with Jardun and Zaedon guarding him. If having the vryndarr nearby was not a deterrent, then Burke standing off to the side with a laser blaster aimed in his direction would be.

My worries about Draejek being a threat had been unfounded. Besides his reluctance to accept help, the male had lost a lot of blood. He was in no condition to offer much of a struggle. I did not have the heart to tell Sloane that her efforts might have been wasted, that when the fight was over, Khyron might decide to end Draejek's life.

By the time she finished, and we had returned to our friends, some of the males standing behind Sarus were looking at Khyron as if genuinely seeing the capable leader he was for the first time. Other than Draejek, who had some kind of leadership role, the remainder of the males were soldiers. They followed Sarus's orders without question, even if they disagreed with them. Khyron showing concern for Draejek's welfare when Sarus disregarded the male as useless had undoubtedly earned him their admiration.

"Draejek?" Khyron asked Sloane.

"He'll live," she said. "But I'm no doctor, so Vurell will need to look at him."

"Thank you." Khyron faced Sarus and pointed his blade at an open area not far from us. "Shall we?"

"Yes," Sarus hissed, the last of his patients dissolving as he took the lead.

The rest of us spread out in a wide circle, our group on one side, Sarus's males on the other. Besides Burke, who continued to stand off to the side and monitor things while armed with the blaster, Khyron and Sarus were the only ones carrying weapons. Everyone else had sheathed their blades shortly after Khyron had given his assurance that no one would interfere.

Sarus didn't wait for anyone to announce the beginning of the fight, nor did he give Khyron a chance to get into position before spinning and swiping at him. Bloodlust filled the older male's sneer, his actions proving once again that he dismissed the use of honor as unnecessary.

Khyron jumped back, but not fast enough to prevent Sarus from slicing through the fabric covering his upper arm. Luckily, the blade only grazed his skin.

Conflict strummed through my system. I had spent years as Khyron's bodyguard. Standing back and doing nothing went against all my training.

After that, the sounds of blades clashing filled the air. Sarus's limp and his lifeless tail did not appear to hinder his fighting skills. He matched Khyron's thrusts and swipes, then lunged, attacking at every available opening, of which there were not many.

As the fight progressed, Laria and Sloane moved closer to Celeste. Cara had also stepped away from Zaedon to rally with her friends. Each female positioned themselves on either side of her, offered their support, and whether they realized it or not, their protection.

Celeste was Khyron's mate, but she was also the drezdarrina, his partner in ruling the planet. A fact that no one had mentioned to Sarus. So even if he managed to end Khyron's life, he would not be able to take on the role of drezdarr as long as Celeste was alive. If it came to that, Jardun, Zaedon, and I would step in to meet any of Sarus's challenges.

The longer they fought, the angrier Sarus became. The more he thirsted for Khyron's blood, the sloppier he got with his aims.

Khyron was fighting the male responsible for his sire's death, yet he fought without emotion, his movements planned and precise.

When Khyron finally got the opening he had been waiting for, he knocked the blade from Sarus's hand, sending it flying through the air and landing several feet away. He crouched and swung out a leg, catching the older male behind the ankles, and causing him to fall backward.

While Sarus lay on his back trying to regain his breath, Khyron pressed the tip of his short sword against his throat. "I will not take your life, but this ends now."

I understood my friend's reason for not putting his relative to death. Revenge never solved anything, nor did it heal the wounds and injustices of the past.

Now that the fight was over, Khyron sheathed his sword as he crossed to the other side of the open space and gathered Celeste in his arms. The males who had followed Sarus seemed uncertain what they should do next. Some talked among themselves, and some milled around.

While the others in my group remained with Khyron, listening to Celeste scold her mate as she examined the cut on his arm, I eased closer to Sarus. I did not trust that the male would take losing gracefully or give up his quest to become the drezdarr.

And my instincts had been right.

Sarus remained on the ground, acting as if he had been too drained from the fight to move. As soon as he thought no one was watching, he rolled onto his hands and knees, then crawled until he reached his sword.

He slowly staggered to his feet, then with renewed strength, headed toward Khyron with his blade aimed at his back.

Memories of the past intertwined with the present. I was not about to watch the sibling of the male I had failed to protect lose his life. I dove at Sarus, attempting to block his killing thrust by wrestling his blade away from him, and ended up with a slice in the flesh along my ribs. The momentum took us both to the ground, the impact with the hard surface sending additional pain along my side.

Sarus was the first to recover and rise to his feet, his eyes flickering with a maniacal gleam. Angered by my interference, he raised his blade and made me his new target.

***

SLOANE

I was relieved when Khyron won the fight but not happy that he'd decided to let Sarus live. It was an honorable thing to do but not a wise decision. His uncle was like a dangerous and deadly creature, never willing to stop until it got what it wanted.

While Khyron had his back turned so he could embrace Celeste, I decided it might be a good idea to keep an eye on Sarus. Garyck must've been thinking the same thing because he'd stepped in front of me and blocked my view.

Only he hadn't stopped to watch. He'd thrown himself at Sarus, who was brandishing a blade and heading for Khyron. He might have saved his friend, but he'd been injured in the process. Blood coated the side of his shirt. He'd also landed on the side where he usually sheathed his knife and struggled to retrieve it.

Sarus wanted Khyron dead, but at the moment, he was more interested in ending Garyck's life.

"No!" I shouted, my feet moving as I drew my new blade. I wouldn't get to Sarus in time to stop him from attacking my mate, but I could reach the end of his tail. Diving the same way Garyck had, only without another person to receive the impact, I landed in the dirt, then drove the knife into limp, scaly flesh. With his tail pinned to the ground, Sarus couldn't reach Garyck, but he could still get to me.

"Female," Sarus roared, pivoting around and raising his blade to strike.

I pulled on my knife, but it didn't want to come out of the ground as easily as it went in, so I gave up trying and rolled to my right, Sarus's swipe missing me by inches.

Before I could get to my feet, Sarus had his blade raised again. At the same time, I was crab-walking backward, I glimpsed movement all around me. It's surprising what you notice when you have fear-induced adrenaline coursing through your system.

Garyck called my name as he clutched his side and raced toward me with Khyron, Jardun, and Zaedon on his heels. Celeste, Laria, and Cara had fallen in behind the males. Sarus had yanked his tail from my blade and stalked toward me, leaving a bloody trail behind him. He had to be in a lot of pain because he was growling like a feral animal.

My head and back slammed into the sun-warmed metal of the transport. I would've rolled over and belly crawled underneath, but Sarus grabbed my ankle and dragged me away from the vehicle.

Just as he was about to plunge his blade into my chest, Draejek appeared and used a sword he must have borrowed from one of the males in his group to block the thrust. Helping me had taken whatever energy he had left because he dropped to his knees. "For your kindness," he said in answer to my questioning gaze.

"Traitor," Sarus snarled, turning his blade on Draejek and driving it into his stomach. It was a killing blow, and as soon as Sarus pulled out his knife, Draejek slumped to the ground. Something inside the older male had snapped. He jumped to his feet and slashed wildly at anyone who got close to him.

Garyck had me by the wrist and pulled me out of harm's way. Everyone else had taken a few steps back to avoid Sarus's blade. His agitated frenzy ended a few minutes later when Burke hit him in the chest with a laser blast that knocked him off his feet, killing him before he hit the ground.

No one would miss Sarus, but I experienced remorse over Draejek's death as I had for Ryan. Their misplaced loyalties had eventually cost them their lives.

I used Garyck's offered hand to climb to my feet. "Little one, are you all right?"

"I'm fine, but you're not." I smacked his hand away when he tried reaching for me. "Let me see." I peeled back his shirt to see how badly he'd been hurt. Garyck winced when I applied pressure to the skin around his wound. There was a nasty gash along his ribs. It had torn through flesh and some of his scales, but it hadn't gone deep enough to cause any significant damage.

"Is he going to make it?" Burke asked as he headed in our direction.

"Yes, but don't you think you could've used that thing a little sooner?" I glanced at the laser weapon, then went back to glaring at Burke.

"I didn't have a clear shot," Burke said, shrugging. "Besides, you looked like you were handling things okay."

I didn't think dragging my backside backward through the dirt qualified as 'handling things', but we were interrupted before I could share my opinion.

"Sloane, what do you think you were doing?" Laria

asked. Her scowl matched the ones on Celeste's and Cara's faces.

I peeled my eyes away from examining Garyck's injury long enough to frown at him. "Saving someone's backside...again."

"Yes, but you got to use your new blade," Garyck said.

I liked hearing the sound of his voice, along with the teasing humor, more than I did his grunts. "Oh yeah, pinning a tail to the ground was an awesome way to see how well it worked," I said sarcastically.

Garyck leaned forward and said, "I will be forever grateful that you did."

"As will I," Khyron said, slipping his arm along the back of Celeste's waist. "To both of you."

Cara opened the medical kit she'd retrieved from the solarveyor. "Here," she said, after handing me a cloth she'd dampened with water so I could clean Garyck's wound.

Once that task was done, I applied healing cream. The ketaurrans hadn't invented an adhesive tape or anything similar, so I had to wrap his broad chest with bandages. Our supply was quickly dwindling, so if anyone else got injured, we'd have to resort to cutting apart clothing.

"Thank you," Garyck pressed a kiss to my forehead.

"You're welcome," I said. "But do you think you can manage to stay out of trouble until we get home?"

"I will do my best." He snorted and pulled me into his arms, wincing when I brushed against his injury.

Since we had an audience, I turned to face away from him. "So," I said to my friends. "What happened to staying behind and protecting the settlement?"

"I'm afraid that was kind of a fib?" Celeste said.

"No kidding," I said, then waited for her to explain.

"We couldn't be sure if Ryan was working alone or if there was someone else in the community he was sharing information with."

"Why didn't you tell me?" I asked, wondering if I had

done something to make my friends think they couldn't share that important detail with me. The hurt must've leaked out in my voice because Laria hurried to say, "Since Ryan was trying to get close to you, we figured the less you knew about the backup plan, the less you'd have to worry about hiding from him."

"So, it wasn't a trust issue then?" I asked.

"Absolutely, not," Celeste huffed.

"And if we'd known you were going to do something as foolish as going off on a solo mission," Laria said, shooting a sidelong glance at Burke. "We definitely would've tried to stop you."

"Then again…" Celeste tapped the band on my arm, leaving the rest of her comment open for interpretation, which wasn't difficult when she included wiggling her brows.

"You did not get lost, did you?" Garyck directed his question at Zaedon and Burke.

"No," Burke said. "We had no idea what we'd run into when we arrived, so we made up the story we told you for the benefit of anyone who might be listening. Turns out, it was a good plan."

"Was Des also privy to your plan?" I asked.

Burke shook his head. "I sent him back to the settlement with instructions to find Khyron. When and if he made it, Logan was supposed to fill him in on what we were doing."

"If it makes you feel any better," Cara said. "Zaedon and I weren't clued into that part of the plan either. Not until Des was gone and Burke told us about meeting up with the others."

Knowing I wasn't the only one who hadn't been privy to the entire plan helped quite a bit. I forced myself to remember that keeping everyone alive was Burke's priority, always had been. He did whatever was necessary to attain that goal, even if it meant bruising others' feelings.

I'd been so busy listening to my friends that I hadn't

noticed one of the males from Sarus's group approach us until he cleared his throat, then said, "Excuse me, drezdarr."

Pale green scales covered his tail and what I could see of his chest and arms. He stood around the same height as Khyron yet kept his demeanor respectful. I didn't get the impression he planned on causing any trouble. With Draejek gone, it appeared the male had been selected to be the spokesperson for the group.

"Yes," Khyron said, shifting to give the male his full attention.

The vryndarr, including Garyck, immediately flanked their friend on both sides. They were his bodyguards first, friends second, so their actions weren't unexpected.

I did, however, wonder why Khyron hadn't addressed Sarus's males before now. Had he purposely given them time to think about what had transpired? Maybe given them a chance to see what true collaboration between the ketaurrans and humans looked like. He was a good leader, and I wouldn't be surprised to learn he'd used both tactics.

"We were curious to know if you have made a decision about our fates," the male asked. The rest of his group had inched closer, moving slowly, so they didn't appear threatening either.

Khyron took a moment before answering. "I have seen way too much bloodshed in my lifetime. I value the lives of every inhabitant on this planet, and my preference would be to avoid any more."

He swept his gaze from one male to the next, studying their expressions as he went. "I will not allow another war." Khyron caressed the hilt of his blade. "If you still support Sarus's misguided ideals and lust for power, we will end it here and now." He paused to let them absorb his words.

Khyron's show of mercy might have been wasted on Sarus, but it wasn't lost on the males who'd followed him. The lead male bowed his head to show respect. "That will not be necessary."

"This place is pretty desolate," I said, remembering the long walk Garyck and I had taken. "Don't you think we should give them a ride?"

Khyron turned back to the male. "Do you require transportation?"

"Thank you, but no," the male said with a hint of a smile. "We have several transports hidden not far from here."

"Then we will leave you to choose a better future." Khyron dismissed the males with a wave of his hand, then to the rest of us, he said, "We have one more task to complete before we leave."

Evening was approaching by the time we finished our so-called task. Khyron, being the honorable male that he was, placed the corpses of Draejek and his uncle, along with the last laser blaster, in the dilapidated building before lighting another fire to ensure no trace of the weapons existed.

If it had been up to me, I would've tossed Sarus's body into a ravine on our way back to the settlement and let the planet's unfriendly creatures enjoy a feast. A fiery funeral was better than the despicable male deserved.

I was about to enter the transport after Laria when Garyck tapped my arm and said, "Wait. I forgot something." He rushed across the compound, disappearing around the corner of the building he and Zaedon had been hiding behind earlier. A few seconds later, he reappeared with my blanket bundle.

"My weapons," I squealed like a child and rose on my toes, brushing a gentle kiss to his lips, and causing his tail to swish. "Thanks for remembering."

He growled when he noticed Jardun and Zaedon standing near a viewing pane, watching us. "Stop grinning unless you think your mates would appreciate a demonstration of the stun stick I have tucked in the folds of this fabric."

They didn't stop grinning, but they did hold up their hands and step away from the pane to give us some privacy. Privacy that turned into a long, drawn-out kiss.

CHAPTER TWENTY

SLOANE

With Des's unexpected arrival and taking on the mission to destroy the blasters, Celeste's wedding plans had been temporarily interrupted. Unfortunately, once we returned to the settlement, no amount of begging or pleading on my part deterred her from making her friends wear dresses for the ceremony.

Harper had found a vendor at the traders market with a collection of outfits people had salvaged when our spaceship had first landed on the planet. Surviving in the current environment required sturdier clothing, so quite a few females had traded in their gowns for more appropriate items.

The dress Celeste and Laria had strong-armed me into selecting fit a little loose and, because of my height, the hem was too long. I'd thought that tripping down the aisle would give me the excuse I needed until Harper had mentioned that her neighbor Jenna had been a talented seamstress before leaving Earth. The female was happy to help and had even done simple alterations for anyone who needed them.

The ceremony had been scheduled to take place outdoors in an area in the forest near Harper and Rygael's place so there would be enough room for everyone in the community to attend. The children under their care, the same ones who balked when asked to clean their rooms, had volunteered to spend the previous day helping with preparations.

Everything seemed to be going as planned. Even the weather was cooperating. So far, not a single cloud dotted the sky.

The males had been shuffled out the door to get ready at the headquarters building not long after everyone had risen for the day. The females used the dwelling I shared with Laria and Celeste for our preparations. My quarters quickly transformed into the hub of our activities. My friends constantly wandered in and out while everyone prepped for the big event.

None of our gowns matched, but they didn't clash either. I'd been afraid the available selection would be limited, and we'd all end up with prints, plaids, and polka dots. Luckily, the vendor had a surplus in varying sizes, so my friends and I could choose outfits in a single shade. Celeste had selected a slim-fitting, pale turquoise gown with thin straps. Laria chose a deep green that matched her eyes. I had gone with a dark blue since my friends refused to let me anything drab.

I might not enjoy wearing dresses, but I still had a hidden feminine side. As I swept my hands down the front of my gown, I couldn't help wonder what Garyck would think when he saw me in it.

He'd moved out of his quarters on the second floor of the headquarters building and had been sharing my room with me. Since our return, Garyck's usual routine of going hunting every morning had changed to spending extra time with me. His grumpy side, which appeared less frequently, had reappeared when Laria made him get up early, then chased him and the rest of the males out so we could get ready.

I grabbed my belt, which still had the sheath and new blade attached to it off a nearby chair. I was about to slip it around my waist when Celeste and Laria strolled into the room. I hadn't bothered shutting the door because it wouldn't have stopped them from entering.

Celeste saw the belt in my hand and rolled her cinnamon eyes. "Don't you dare even think about putting that thing on."

"You're letting the guys wear their blades," I said, clutching the belt and blade to my chest because I didn't trust my friend not to snatch it away from me. "Why can't I wear mine?"

"Because that particular accessory doesn't go with your dress," Celeste said.

"You're using fashion as an excuse…seriously."

"My wedding, my rules."

"But I feel naked without my blade," I whined one last time before tossing it on the bed.

"Please," Laria said. "We all know you have a dagger stashed in your boot." She bent over and lifted the hem of her dress to do the same thing with her thin blade.

I hated that she knew me so well. After pulling on my boots, the dagger was the first thing I'd added to my ensemble.

Celeste walked over to me and placed her hands on my shoulders. "I know how much you hate dressing up, and I appreciate you doing this for me."

My feminine side was getting the better of me today because her touching words had moisture building in my eyes. I was spared the embarrassment of crying, something I never did in front of my friends, by Cara, who'd picked that moment to peek her head into the room. "Hey," she said. "If you guys are done with the mushy girl talk, we need to get going, or we're going to be late."

I'd left my hair down rather than pulling it back in a braid. After giving the curls an extra fluff, I sucked in a breath, then said, "Geez, they're already mated. It's not like he's going to leave her standing at the altar."

"Sloane." My friends drew out my name as if they'd rehearsed it just for today.

"What?" I giggled, hiking up my skirt as I hurried through the doorway ahead of them.

***

GARYCK

I already knew what to expect during the human wedding ceremony, yet I could not ease my anxiety. A clearing in the wooded area near the outskirts of the community had been chosen for the event. Makeshift benches, lined up in two rows with an aisle running between them, were already filling with guests. Khyron, Jardun, Zaedon, and I stood opposite the spot where Vince would stand to officiate the ceremony.

My friends and I had participated in a rehearsal the evening before, which turned out to be an enactment of the actual ritual. Shortly before Sloane disappeared to spend the morning preparing with her friends, she had informed me that getting ready for a wedding was almost as important as the event itself.

Not long after our arrival in the wooded clearing, Harper had instructed Jardun, Zaedon, and me to wait with Khyron until she signaled us that the ceremony was ready to start. Then we would be joining our mates to walk with them down the aisle.

For a male who usually handled all tasks and objectives calmly, Khyron seemed to be doing worse than me. It was unusual to glimpse even the slightest amount of nervousness in his demeanor, yet faced with his upcoming nuptials had him pacing.

The male was already mated, so I was unsure what was worrying him.

"Khyron," Jardun said. "Are you regretting your decision to have a human wedding?"

"What?" Khyron jerked his head away from staring at the opposite end of the aisle. "No. Why would you ask such a thing?"

Jardun glanced at Khyron's feet, which he was shuffling back and forth.

Khyron growled and immediately stopped moving.

Gabe and Ben, two of the young males in Harper's care, were perched on the bench closest to us. Gabe held up his hand, pretending to disguise what he was saying to Ben. "Maybe he thinks Celeste won't show up." Both young ones giggled, earning a stern glare from Khyron, making them laugh even more. Encouraging the small males would only make things worse, so I clamped my lips to hide my amusement.

"Hush, you two," Harper said, rounding the end of their bench. She scrunched her face into a stern motherly expression. "Or I'll make you sit in the back." To us, she said, "It's time. Khyron, you stay here. Vince will be joining you in a few minutes. The rest of you follow me." She hooked a finger, ordering us the same way she did the children.

Minutes after we reached the back of the clearing, the others participating in the ceremony arrived.

"Hey," Sloane said, stepping around the group to stand next to me. She caressed my arm with her warm hand.

"Hey back," I said, taking a deep whiff of her alluring scent and letting my gaze travel over every inch of her. Radiant did not begin to describe my ketiorra's beauty. Her hair was down, the dark curls draping her shoulders. "You are beautiful," I murmured, unsure why wearing the garment had bothered her.

She had refused to wear the dress for me or let me examine it before today. The blue fabric that highlighted her eyes was a bit loose but fit her curves perfectly.

"Thanks," Sloane said, the flush on her cheeks making

me happy. "Are you ready?"

"I believe so," I said, wishing the ceremony was over so I could whisk her away and take my time removing the garment from her body.

"Okay, everyone, let's get started," Harper said. "Melissa, Lily, you go first with Draejill."

Lily gave Harper a we-know-what-to-do look, then aimed the youngest of the children Harper had adopted toward the aisle.

Draejill was half-human, half-ketaurran. With pale tangerine scales and golden hair, he was also the most adorable.

Fuzzball, who had not been part of the rehearsal, had managed to sneak past us so he could follow the young ones. "It's okay," Celeste said, stopping Harper from racing after him.

Draejill found picking up the chirayka flowers Melissa and Lily sprinkled on the ground from their baskets as they walked, more interesting than following them. His antics were even more entertaining when he plopped down in the middle of the dirt path and started eating the deep purple blossoms. Fuzzball assumed the child wanted to play and joined him.

"Draejill," Melissa huffed. She and Lily each took one of his small hands and helped him off the ground and down the remainder of the aisle where Harper's friend Jenna was waiting to pick him up.

Laria and Jardun went next, then Cara and Zaedon. Sloane and I were the next in line. All my vryndarr training, and the stealth that accompanied it, disappeared the instant Sloane tucked her arm in mine.

It was hard to focus on the aisle when my gaze kept seeking my mate. Halfway to the other end, my knee caught the edge of a bench. Because I was not paying attention to my tail, which had been swishing from the moment Sloane arrived, I ended up getting the tip accidentally stepped on by a guest.

"Garyck," Sloane whispered when we reached our destination, and I did not release her. She nudged me hard with her hip. "You need to let me go, remember?"

I had no problem recalling what I was supposed to do. I did not understand the purpose of joining the males when I preferred to remain with my mate.

"If you go, I promise to let you examine my dress more thoroughly later," she said.

Sloane's incentive included more than merely touching the fabric of her gown. It was an invitation to remove the garment from her gorgeous body and share her bed, an enticement I could not refuse. I responded with a grunt to let her know I accepted her offer, then took the empty spot next to my friends.

If Khyron had witnessed the exchange, he did not say anything. He was too busy watching Celeste being escorted down the aisle by Vurell. The older male wore a solemn expression, proudly puffing out his chest and straightening his shoulders as he walked.

Celeste had no living relatives, so she had asked Vurell to take on her sire's role and perform the duty of giving her away. Since she was already bonded to Khyron, I did not understand the human concept, so I kept my views about the act being moot to myself.

Once Celeste and Khyron stood next to each other in front of Vince, everything progressed quickly. Either that or I was too busy watching Sloane to pay attention to the activities. I had noticed that Fuzzball only attacked Khyron's tail once during the ceremony, which was an improvement for the small creature. The young ones had been training him to behave, but he still needed more work.

Before long, my friends and I, along with many people from the community, had migrated to the gathering room of the headquarters building.

Thanks to Sloane, my comfort level around a large group of people was getting better, but I still preferred to linger near the outskirts and close to the door. My mate had recently gotten containers of ale for both of us and was leaning against the wall with me when Melissa popped out of a nearby crowd.

"Garyck," she said, tipping her head back to look up at me. "I'm glad I didn't have to give you the talk."

"Me as well," I said. I remembered the first time the child had approached me about the same subject. I had no more clarity now than I did then. Once the child walked away and was not within earshot, I raised a brow at Sloane and asked, "Talk?"

Sloane laughed. "Apparently, she is good at advising males who are clueless when it comes to winning the hearts of their ketiorras." She smiled and winked. "It's a good thing you figured it out all by yourself."

Her mischievous tone reminded me of her earlier comment regarding her gown, a promise I was looking forward to receiving. I took the half-empty container from her hand and placed it on a corner table along with mine.

"Hey, I wasn't finished with that," she said.

I blocked her attempt to grab it back. "I do not think anyone will miss us if we leave, do you?"

"I'm pretty sure they…" Sloane squealed as I hefted her over my shoulder. Other than a few snorts and chuckles, the noise around us faded.

"Garyck," Khyron called from the opposite side of the room where he stood with Celeste tucked against his side. The male appeared more relaxed and content than I had seen him in years. "I assume everything is all right."

"Everything is wonderful," I said, genuinely meaning it as I opened the door and stepped onto the porch, the laughter of my friends, along with Sloane's, filling the evening air.

For the first time in a very long time, the prospect of a happy future, one without the threat of war, awaited me in the arms of my ketiorra.

GARYCK'S GIFT

<<<<>>>>

ABOUT THE AUTHOR

Rayna Tyler is an author of paranormal and sci-fi romance. She loves writing about strong sexy heroes and the sassy heroines who turn their lives upside down. Whether it's in outer space or in a supernatural world here on Earth, there's always a story filled with adventure.

Made in United States
Troutdale, OR
02/16/2024